The Temple of the Blind

Book Three

The Temple of the Blind

Brian Harmon

The Temple of the Blind

Published by Brian Harmon

Cover Image and Design by Brian Harmon

ISBN: 1466226188
ISBN-13: 978-1466226180

Also by Brian Harmon

The Box
(Book One of The Temple of the Blind)

Gilbert House
(Book Two of The Temple of the Blind)

For Nathan

Chapter 1

The cellar door stood open at the far end of the tunnel, the last of the day's sunlight pouring down from above, welcoming them back from the hell they had somehow endured.

Wayne Oakley stopped and gazed back into the darkness one final time before climbing the steps. Back there was Gilbert House, in all its impossible, sprawling madness. There was a monster in there somewhere, a pale, hulking, murdering thing, but he felt that another monster had come back with them, a monster that made promises and did not keep them, who offered protection when he could not deliver.

A warm hand slipped into his as he gazed despondently back, and he turned to meet Nicole Smart's sympathetic eyes. "I'm sorry about Olivia." He knew by the sadness on her face that she was sincere, but it did not change how awful he felt. How could he have failed so completely? He doubted if he would ever forget the sound of the poor girl's terrified screams as she was sucked into that awful darkness.

"We're all sorry," agreed Albert as he and Brandy started up the steps.

Nicole tugged softly at his hand and he began to move again, willingly following her up the steps and out of the nightmare.

Here, as the four of them squinted into the dwindling evening sunlight, they were greeted by a startling sound. It was the slow and repetitive concussion of a single pair of hands clapping together.

"Impressive." The woman appeared to be in her late forties or early fifties. She was standing in the deepening shadows beneath a nearby tree. She was skinny, almost unhealthily so, and her raven black hair was likewise fine, flat and limp. Her face still retained remnants of a beauty that she must have possessed in her youth, but her dark eyes were framed by fine lines. She wore very little makeup, if any, and was dressed in loose-fitting khaki pants and a black, short-sleeve shirt. “When I heard the screaming, I thought for sure you wouldn’t come back.”

“Who are you?” Albert demanded.

The woman smiled at him, but it was not a pleasant smile. “Beverly Bridger, as if you didn’t know.”

Albert stared at her, confused. As if he didn’t know? He had never seen this woman before in his life.

“I think you have something of mine.”

“I do?”

Beverly glared at him. As he gazed back at her, he found something about her eyes oddly unsettling. “My file?”

“Your file…?” Albert realized that she meant the envelope. When Andrea Prophett gave him the envelope, she told him that someone sneaked up to her window in the middle of the night and taped it to the screen. Was Beverly the mystery courier? Now that he thought about it, Olivia had informed them that an older woman was waiting for them when she and her friends showed up here Wednesday evening. That woman, she’d told them, gave her boyfriend a letter that sounded exactly like the one Wayne received the same day. Beverly fit the description perfectly.

"I don't know how you did it, and I don't want to know. I don't care. I just want some answers." There was a gleam in her eyes that Albert didn't care for at all, like girlish glee tainted with strained desperation.

"What are you talking about?" Albert asked.

Beverly ignored him and turned her eyes to Wayne. "I didn't think I'd see *you* again."

"You gave me my letter, too?"

Beverly nodded. "You were one of three. Only one of you showed up the night you were supposed to."

Wayne barely suppressed a shiver. Three of them? He wondered who the third was. "Why me?"

"Why *you*? Look at you. Gilbert House isn't safe. I needed someone big and strong, someone tough enough to get in and back out."

"Then why me?" asked Albert. He liked to think that he was pretty tough, especially since his trip to the Temple of the Blind last year, but he knew he certainly didn't *look* as formidable as Wayne.

Beverly looked at him, less amused than shocked.

"What do you mean, 'Why me?'" she snarled.

"I don't..." Albert shook his head, confused. "You sent me that envelope, didn't you?"

Beverly's expression shifted to shock and then to anger. "*Sent* it to you? You *stole* it from me!"

"What?" This was from Brandy. "You're fucking crazy."

"A girl dropped it off at my house this afternoon," Albert explained. "She said someone taped it to her window in the middle of the night." His voice was calm, not defensive, but it set her off nonetheless.

"*Don't lie to me*!" snapped Beverly. "No one else knew about my file!"

Albert looked at Brandy, confused. When he looked back, he said. "You don't even know me."

Beverly's eyes were sharp and stabbing. "You're Albert Cross." She spoke both his names as though they were vulgarities, almost spitting them at him.

"How do you know him?" asked Nicole.

Beverly did not look at her. She only stared straight at Albert, as though half expecting him to lunge at her. "I know where he was last September," she said, as if she were revealing some filthy secret.

Albert and Brandy looked at each other, surprised. "How did you know we were down there?"

"I saw it," Beverly replied.

"You *saw* it?" Brandy asked, horrified by the idea of anyone seeing the things they'd done in those dark chambers.

"Dreamt it, actually," Beverly clarified. "Look, I didn't camp out up here for the past three days to talk about you people. Now tell me what you found!"

The four of them exchanged worried looks. This conversation was becoming very uncomfortable.

"What's so special about this place?" Albert asked, avoiding her question. "Why do you want to know about it so bad? And why not just go in and see for yourself?"

The woman's expression hardened, her eyes narrowing. It was clear that she possessed little patience, but she granted them her reply. "It's special to me because it's been torturing me my whole life. I feel it every day. It's like poison ivy that won't go away. It just keeps itching and itching but you can't scratch it."

"And you want us to scratch it for you," Albert said.

His tone was intentionally mocking. He did not like this Beverly Bridger any more than he had liked Gilbert House's squat bouncer.

"Yes," Beverly replied, clearly losing her patience now. "I want you to scratch it for me. *Now tell me what you found, you little freak*!"

"You keep talking to him like that, bitch" said Nicole, "and I'll kick your fucking teeth in."

Beverly shot her a hateful look, but only briefly. Her eyes fluttered immediately back to Albert as though she expected him to charge her at any moment.

Albert glanced at his friend, surprised. He'd never heard Nicole stand up for him like that. But then again, he'd never been confronted like this in front of her before, either. For that matter, he'd never been confronted like this at all.

He stared at Beverly for a moment without speaking, considering the situation. He did not like this woman at all, and he'd begun to doubt her sanity besides.

"I don't know if we should," Wayne said. "I don't trust her."

Beverly glared at him, her dark eyes hateful.

"Yeah," Albert replied. "I know."

"Let's just go, guys," Brandy pleaded.

Albert could see the woman's rage growing. "You never told us why you couldn't just go in and see for yourself," he reminded her, further pushing her tolerance.

Beverly seemed to have to draw all her mental strength to calm herself. Through clenched teeth, she replied, "I just *can't*."

"Why?"

The woman growled, frustrated. "*Just tell me what you saw*!"

"You sent four people in there Wednesday night," Wayne said, and Albert was pleased to hear the fury in his voice. "None of them came out and you still let us go in there. Now you expect us to tell you what we saw?" He stepped forward, brushing past Albert.

Beverly took a step backward, obviously afraid of him and rightfully so. Wayne clearly outweighed her significantly.

"Because of you, they're all *dead*! And all you care about is what we saw?"

"*I did what I had to do!*" Beverly screamed at him.

This was clearly the wrong reply because Wayne's eyes suddenly grew very large. With speed uncharacteristic of his size, he lunged forward and grabbed the woman before she could turn and flee.

Albert's heart leapt when he heard the woman scream. He did not know what was about to happen, but he could not imagine any good coming from it.

Wayne hauled the skinny woman off the ground and over one shoulder. She shrieked as if she were being murdered—and perhaps that was exactly what she thought was happening. He spun around, hardly noticing the wild kicking of the woman he now held like a sack of laundry. "You want to know what's inside there? I'll show you!" In the wake of his grief and fury, he wanted to carry her all the way to the farthest corner of the basement. He wanted to drop her behind the door and then pile the cinderblocks in front of it and leave her there to suffer the fate to which she'd doomed Olivia's friends two days ago. The sound of her pleading and begging behind that door would be horribly satisfying.

But when he began to walk toward the cellar door, the woman went crazy. She screamed to be let down, shrieked so loudly the whole city must have heard her, as though she'd read the terrible thoughts straight from his brain.

Brandy and Nicole both clapped their hands over their mouths and watched in disbelief as the woman came apart in Wayne's grip.

Albert wanted to stop him, wanted to tell him to just put the woman down before she shrieked herself into cardiac arrest or something, but he was frozen in place, too shocked to speak.

Fortunately for Beverly, Wayne's determination to send her into the hell she'd served to Olivia was not quite as strong as her utter terror of it. She pounded him with her fists and kicked and thrashed and when her balance finally began to topple, she grabbed a handful of his thick, black hair and yanked so hard she actually tore a lock of it out. He cried out in pain and then stooped and dropped her.

As soon as her feet hit the ground she tried to run away, but it was no good. Before she could escape his reach, he seized her by her shirt.

Albert would later remember the moment in vivid

detail. Wayne held onto the back of Beverly's shirt with both hands and spun her like an oversized doll. She actually came off the ground as she sailed almost a full three hundred sixty degrees. There was a loud pop that was the sound of all the buttons on her shirt letting go at once. And when Wayne released her, she flew through the air for a brief moment before her feet touched the ground and she toppled forward into a thick patch of thorny brush.

Wayne growled and started toward her again, still hell bent on dragging her into Gilbert House.

"Wayne, stop!" Albert called, finally finding his voice. And to his surprise, Wayne *did* stop. "She's done! Don't hurt her."

"Any more," added Nicole. She could not believe she'd just witnessed such a spectacle.

Beverly lay in the brush, sobbing into the dirt. Her shoulders ached, her knees and hands stung and her wrist was throbbing.

"Come on, everybody," Albert said. "We should go."

"Wait!" Beverly pushed herself up and rolled over onto her back. Her shirt fell open and her white, silky bra shimmered in the diminishing daylight. She did not try to hide herself. There was a shallow cut on her belly and another on her cheek. She held her left wrist in her right hand as though comforting a pain. "Tell me!"

"I can't believe it!" Wayne hissed and Beverly shrank away from him at the sound of his fury. No one there could have blamed her.

"Forget about it," Albert told him. He looked at the woman, surprised she could even speak after being flung around like that, much less that she still possessed the audacity to push the very subject that had enraged Wayne in the first place. "Do you need help?"

Beverly shook her head. "I need to *know*," she said. "*Please*!"

"Monsters," he told her. "There are monsters in there." He took Brandy's hand and the two of them walked away.

Nicole stared at Beverly for a moment and then followed her friends.

Wayne lingered the longest. He stood staring at her, hating her and pitying her at the same time. "I'm sorry," he said flatly, and then he too walked away. He wouldn't have really locked her inside to die. He merely wanted her to grasp the horrors she had brought upon innocent people. It was her fault they were dead. She deserved to feel worse than he did, and he felt like nothing less than a murderer.

They left Gilbert House behind as the sun sank low behind the trees. Behind them, Beverly Bridger began to sob again.

Chapter 2

Andrea Prophett watched in amazement as the drama unfolded before her eyes. Albert and his friends were walking away now, vanishing into the trees from which they'd come.

The older woman was still lying in the brush. She could hear her weeping, soft and long, pitiful. For a moment she actually thought that guy was going to kill her.

Rachel was never going to believe this.

She had no idea what went on inside Gilbert House, but twice she'd heard screaming. Strangely enough, it seemed to her that the screams were coming not from underground or from the hole by which they'd entered, but from somewhere above her, from somewhere over those creepy, windowless walls. But of course that had only been her imagination. Wherever they'd gone, something bad happened in there, something scary…and did Albert say something about monsters before he left? She thought that was the word he used, but she couldn't really hear him from where she was hiding.

After the four of them had been gone for a moment, the older woman stood up and left in the same direction. Andrea waited until she was out of sight and then followed after them as well.

She kept to the trees, circling the clearing, aware that there could still be more people hidden in these woods. She wanted to move faster, to catch up with everyone, to see where they were going, but she did not dare risk being seen. Not after what happened to that woman.

By the time she reached the parking lot of H & M Tires, there was no one in sight. Even the woman had vanished. They must have all been parked down here somewhere and she was too slow to catch up to them before they drove away.

For a moment she lingered, disappointed. It was all

over now. She doubted that any of them would be back anytime soon, and she knew little more than she did when that envelope first appeared at her window.

She thought about the cellar door. She could sneak inside while no one was around and see for herself where they had gone. There must be some kind of room down there or something, someplace where they had spent all that time. Perhaps the answer to this whole weird mystery was right at the bottom of those steps.

She started back up the hill, not toward Gilbert House, but toward home. She knew she did not possess the courage it would take to go down into that creepy hole, especially with night falling. Maybe tomorrow she could gather the nerve to sneak inside, but not now. These woods were already giving her the creeps.

But as she approached the clearing where Gilbert House stood, she abruptly stopped. Something was there. A large, pale shape loomed in front of the cellar door. It looked vaguely human, but horribly disproportioned. It stood facing away from her, revealing only its broad, fleshy back in the fading daylight, but she saw enough to fill her instantly with icy terror.

Without warning, all the strength left her body. She fell forward onto the forest floor, suddenly and completely paralyzed. She tried to cry out, to scream, but nothing would come. She could not make her voice work. She could not even blink.

"Don't be afraid." The voice came not from any particular direction, but from everywhere at once, as though it were all around her. It was the voice of a man, but different from any man's voice she'd ever heard before. It was deep and small, gentle and yet strong. It seemed coarse and gravelly, but also somehow musical.

She tried to ask who was there, but the words would not come. She could not even move her tongue. It lay useless against her teeth.

"Who I am is not important. Relax. Wait. The creature is leaving, moving away from you."

The *creature*? What did it mean by "creature"? What *was* that thing by the cellar door?

What's happening to me? Unable to form words, all she could do was think these things, but the strange, alien voice could apparently read her mind.

"You will be fine, but you must remain still. If it sees

you, it will kill you."

Fresh terror rushed through her.

"Relax," said the mysterious voice again, and somehow she did relax. There was something soothing about the voice and she found herself embracing it. "It will be gone in a moment and it will not return. In the meantime, I need you to listen very closely to what I have to say. Lives depend on you."

Chapter 3

"Do you think he hurt her?" Brandy sat in the front passenger seat of Albert's aging Ford. Nicole and Wayne had climbed into the cramped back seat.

"I don't know," replied Albert.

"She obviously wasn't that hurt if she was still demanding to know what we saw," Nicole said. She reached over and touched Wayne's hand. He had been staring silently out the window. He looked at her, gave her a pitiful, half-attempt at a smile and then turned away again.

"She really didn't want to go in there," Albert said, pondering. "She flipped out when he carried her toward the door."

"How could she be so obsessed with that place and not want to go inside?" Brandy wondered. "It doesn't make sense."

"No, it doesn't." Albert pulled onto Redwood Avenue, which bisected the campus at an angle from northwest to southeast. It was still fairly early, and the campus would still be crawling with students for another couple of hours, but they might get lucky. With Wayne's help, they should be able to move the cover off the service tunnel entrance, get in and cover it back over relatively quickly.

"I think she was just nuts," Nicole said. "We're probably lucky she didn't pull a gun on us or something."

Albert had already thought about this. Considering how desperate she'd been to learn what they found, it seemed surprising that she wasn't armed, especially considering that there were four of them and only one of her. She'd also been directly involved in the deaths of four people. With something like that on your hands, why not go ahead and get the information you want at gunpoint?

"I've never attacked anyone like that," Wayne said

miserably. "I swear I'm never that violent."

"Forget it," Albert said. "Not your fault."

Brandy agreed. "You were upset over Olivia. We all were, and she was just begging for it."

"Still, I shouldn't have done that. I shouldn't have *thrown* her like that!"

Nicole gave his hand another reassuring squeeze.

"It's not like you punched her out," Brandy said.

"She sent her in there," Wayne continued. He was talking about Olivia. "She sent all of them in there. She killed them all." He turned away from the window and looked at Nicole. "And she *knew* it wasn't safe. She *told* me it wasn't safe. She told me that's why she picked me. Because I was *big*."

Not big enough, Albert thought. The memory of that monster lifting Wayne by his head in one huge hand made him shudder.

"I can't believe she'd even show her face," Nicole said. "We could totally go to the police if we wanted, tell them about her crazy letters and how we found bodies in there."

"They wouldn't believe us," said Brandy.

“She seemed to think I already knew who she was,” Albert remembered. “Maybe she approached us because she thought we already knew she was there.”

“If we went to the police and told them about the envelopes,” pressed Nicole, “and just that we went into Gilbert House through that cellar door and found the bodies, if we said nothing about the rest of it, they’d have no reason not to check it out. Then they’d see everything for themselves.”

“That’s true.” Brandy turned to Albert. “I wonder if we *should* tell someone.”

Albert wasn’t paying attention. He was thinking about Beverly Bridger and the hostility with which she’d approached them. Why no weapon? Why all the secrecy? It didn’t make sense. And what was with her accusing him of stealing her file?

“I don’t know,” said Nicole. “It seems wrong to just leave those people in there and not tell anybody where they are.”

“Gilbert House should be forgotten,” said Wayne as he gazed out the window. “Wherever we were when we were in there, I don’t think people were meant to go there."

"He's got a point," Albert said. "Do you know how many police officers and crime scene investigators would have to go in there if we told them where to find those bodies? And then who gets involved? Scientists? The military?"

"So we should just leave them there?" Nicole asked, her voice understandably doubtful.

Albert shook his head. "I don't know. We should go to the temple first. Maybe then we'll know what to do." He turned off of Redwood and onto Third Street, and drove south toward Jackson Street. "I wonder what she knows. She knew about the temple, said she *dreamt* it."

"Do you think she was there?" Brandy asked. A shiver ran through her at the thought. It was terrifying to think that they could have been watched the whole time they were down there. And if Beverly had seen them, could someone else have seen them too? How many pairs of eyes could have been on them as they roamed those dark corridors? She remembered the things she and Albert did inside the sex room and the thought of someone standing in the dark, watching the whole thing… It was mortifying.

Albert considered the idea. “I don’t see how.” It was awful dark down there, but it would have been difficult to stay out of sight and not get lost or stumble into a trap. He supposed it would be possible, however, assuming someone knew the corridors well enough.

“Do you think she really dreamed it?” Brandy sounded skeptical, but she knew better than to dismiss anything. Nothing was impossible. The temple had taught her that.

Albert shook his head. He had no idea. The woman was an enigma to him, as mysterious as the wooden box that first brought him into these bizarre worlds thirteen months ago.

He turned west onto Jackson Street. The nearest place to park to the service tunnel entrance was the south parking lot, by the stadium.

“Maybe she did,” Nicole said. “It wouldn’t be much different from the phone calls you two were getting.”

“I guess that’s true,” Albert agreed.

“Phone calls?” Wayne inquired.

Albert forgot that Wayne still knew very little about

his and Brandy's experiences with the temple. "I told you that we found the temple last year…"

Wayne recalled that Albert had referred to it as "the Temple of the Blind."

"Last night, we started getting these strange phone calls. We'd pick up and nobody was there. It was just silence, except that while we listened, we kept remembering things we saw down there. Really strong mental images. It felt like we were being called back. Then we got the envelope and I figured they must be connected, but so far I haven't seen how."

"So you think those phone calls were…what? Some sort of psychic telegraphs?"

"Yeah. Just like that."

"Weird."

"Not the weirdest thing you've seen or heard today," Nicole pointed out.

"True." He no longer doubted anything that Albert told him. Between the monster that nearly crushed his skull and the dark forest and five-story building that only existed on one side of an old cellar door, his former perception of what was possible had already been obliterated. He now fully believed that there were men with no eyes and underground chambers designed to make him fear and hate uncontrollably.

Albert pulled into the south parking lot via its northeast drive and drove west, along the northern edge. The signs read simply "Perimeter Parking" and "Any Permit," but it was commonly referred to as "the south lot" or "the big lot". It was huge, stretching back into the forest and wrapping around behind the college stadium. This was the lot where people parked when they were not lucky enough to get a good parking permit. It was not terribly far from Happens, Juggers or the field house, which was fine if you happened to be an art, music or physical education major, but if you majored in anything else, you had to expect a hike.

"Thanks for bringing me along, guys," Wayne said. Nicole had taken her hand from his and was staring out the window toward Juggers Hall. Behind it was the place Albert and Brandy told her about, the place where they're great adventure began. She could not believe she was finally going there.

"Don't thank us yet," Albert said. "It's just as

dangerous down there as it was in Gilbert House. Maybe more so. You can still change your mind, if you want."

Wayne shook his head. "No. I want to come. You said you came to Gilbert House because you thought it had something to do with what you found down there. Maybe it does. If so I want to know."

Albert nodded. "Then welcome aboard." He found a spot in the third row from the stadium and parked the car.

"Besides," Nicole added, "if we run into anything we don't like, he can rough it up for us."

Albert chuckled. "I thought for a second you were going to toss her right down the cellar steps, like it or not."

"That's so bad," Brandy giggled. "I hope she's all right."

"So do I," said Wayne. There was no humor in his voice.

Chapter 4

By the time the four of them arrived at the back steps of Juggers Hall, darkness had fallen and there were only two people within sight of the tunnel's entrance.

"Doesn't look too bad," said Wayne, as he eyed the two students nervously. He'd never done anything like this before. He couldn't help but wonder how many rules they were about to break.

"Doesn't look bad at all," Albert agreed. "I expected a lot more people to be out, especially on a Friday night." He looked at his watch. "It's still early."

"Maybe people don't want to hang out on dark campus sidewalks on a Friday night," suggested Nicole. She stared at the metal plate that covered the service tunnel entrance. She'd walked right over that spot countless times since Albert and Brandy first told her the story, and each time she could not help but think of all the wondrous things she knew lay somewhere beneath it. She'd wanted so badly for so long to go down there and now she was finally getting her chance. It was almost more than she could stand.

They stood and watched as the two students walked away from them. They were young men, dressed in workout clothes. They were probably on their way home from the field house. Neither paid them any attention and when they were gone, only the four of them remained. The entire area was deserted and the only sound was the soft, droning roar of the nearby power plant.

"We should do it fast," Wayne said.

As the four of them walked to the tunnel's entrance, Albert recalled the first time he moved that heavy, metal cover. He and Brandy had nearly been spotted by a group of students who happened to walk by. He remembered standing silently in the darkness below, waiting for them to leave, his skin crawling at the thought of unseen things slithering and slinking toward him. It had been an awful experience, and he certainly didn't want to relive it tonight. This time, they would be quicker.

Albert and Wayne lifted the cover and each of them descended into the darkness before another pedestrian could wander by.

"Well," said Wayne after the cover was securely replaced above his head. "We're in the sewers. Now what?"

Albert turned on his flashlight and began to walk toward the power plant as he studied the wall. "Brandy marked these walls last time. If the paint's still here, we won't need the map."

"Sound's like a plan," said Wayne. "So *is* it still there?"

Albert continued to search. For a moment he thought it was not, that it had either faded during the past thirteen months or that someone had come along and cleaned it off, but then he found it, marking the first turn down a sloping tunnel to the left. "Here it is," he announced. "Let's go."

The past few weeks in Briar Hills had been rainy and the tunnels were considerably wetter than they were the first time Albert and Brandy traveled them. The first time, almost everything had been damp, but now small pools of water stood in many of the tunnels and the smell of mildew and decay was much worse.

They spoke little as they walked, each of them anxious and thoughtful as they wondered what awaited them ahead.

Everything was vividly familiar to Albert, as though it had only been yesterday that he and Brandy ventured these spooky corridors together. But this time, knowing where they were going and eager to get there, everything passed almost in a blur as he pushed on and on, past the steam tunnels and into the deeper, colder passages beyond.

Like last time, he found himself dwelling on the complexity of these tunnels. Did Briar Hills really need so many tunnels? Was there really a purpose for each of these passages? It just didn't seem to match the simplicity of the streets and buildings above.

Wayne thought nothing of the massive tangle of tunnels. He barely even noticed them as he walked. He dwelled on the events of the day instead. He remembered that morning, so many long, long hours before, how he'd nearly slept with his roommate's girlfriend. God, but that seemed like so long ago. *Days* ago. He remembered walking away from her, feeling as though he'd won, that he'd proven himself a decent and honest person, but right now he didn't feel like it. He'd promised Olivia Shadey that he'd take care of her, promised her he wouldn't let anything happen to her, and he failed her. He'd tried his best. He'd done all he could to keep her safe. He even stood between her and that monster. He physically placed himself in front of her. He almost *died* for her. How could he have known that there was something else, something bigger, something worse, that would creep up from behind them and snatch her away like that? But still he was haunted by the fact that he'd failed to keep his promise to her. It seemed he wasn't very good at keeping promises, no matter how good his intentions were. Now she would never be married, would never have a child, would never live out her dreams, whatever they may have been. It was a tragedy. And it was his fault.

But that was behind him now. No matter how bad he felt, he couldn't just turn around and crawl home. He had to keep going. He wasn't here to prove anything to anyone. He wasn't here for some grand adventure. He wasn't even here to avenge Olivia Shadey. It was too late for that. The dead were dead. He came here for himself, to at least try and understand why. And also because he had seen between those great, stubby fingers what really happened in that third floor hallway.

Albert Cross had nearly died next to him, not because he couldn't get away, but because he threw himself at the monster in a futile attempt to save Wayne's life. *His. Wayne Oakley's.* A *nobody* he'd only just met. Even through the pain of those great, machine-like fingers squeezing his skull, he'd seen how Albert risked his life to save him when he and the girls could have made a run for it, *should* have made a run for it.

These were good people. He'd already seen enough to know it. Nicole Smart was kind to him, had comforted him in the car, had stood up for him for what he did to that crazy woman outside Gilbert House. Brandy and Nicole had both tried so hard to take care of Olivia when they regrouped, and he remembered seeing the compassion in their eyes, the depth of their sincerity. He remembered the way Brandy Rudman held Olivia's hand as they made their way through the hall, trying to escape.

He'd been doubtful about them at first. Albert had come off arrogant and snotty as they explored the basement, but Wayne soon realized that it was not arrogance but confidence, and he was not a bit snotty, but rather thoughtful, alert, aware. He was a very intelligent person. And the girls had turned out to be strong and smart and kind. These were three very good people, and he'd be damned if they were going anywhere a fraction as dangerous as Wendell Gilbert's hell house without him. Besides, perhaps this was where his life had always been leading him. Perhaps these dark tunnels were where God always intended him to be.

From somewhere up ahead, they heard the sound of running water, as though they were approaching a creek in the woods instead of ducking through underground tunnels, and Albert knew immediately what was in store. Thirteen months ago he and Brandy begrudgingly waded through a pool of standing water in one of these tunnels. This time the rains had turned the tunnel into an underground stream.

Brandy growled, frustrated. “I hate this tunnel!”

“Come on,” Albert said. It’s running water this time. It’s got to be cleaner.” Indeed, the garbage that had lain strewn across the bottom the previous year was gone, washed away in the current. The only rubbish to be seen was the occasional scrap of litter emerging from one darkness and vanishing into the next.

“In the sewers?” Nicole was skeptical.

“It’s just runoff from the streets,” Albert explained. He stepped off into the water and sucked in his breath. It was deeper than before and felt as cold as ice. “Come on everybody. We’re almost there.”

Brandy stepped into the flooded tunnel with a groan and Nicole followed. She made a pitiful whining noise in her throat as her socks soaked up the cold water.

Wayne stepped in after them without hesitating. “Oh yeah!” he hissed. “That’s cold.”

Albert shined his light ahead. “We’re just going right down there.”

“Even runoff is dirty,” Nicole said, grimacing at the feel of the cold, disgusting water on her feet.

“I’m sorry,” said Albert.

"It's okay." And it was. Nicole had wanted to come and see Albert and Brandy's Temple of the Blind since she first heard the story and now she was finally getting her chance. There was no way in hell she was going to turn back because of water, whether it was spring water, runoff or raw sewage.

The four of them stepped into the next tunnel, which was mercifully dry, and made their way to the next. One by one, they crawled the tight, narrow passage to the hole that allowed access to the final tunnel between them and the Temple of the Blind.

"Wow," said Wayne. "How old do you suppose this tunnel is?"

"I'm guessing this is the original one," Albert replied. "As old as the temple itself."

"And how old do you think that is?" Nicole asked.

Albert shook his head. "No way to know," he replied.

About seventy yards ahead, the tunnel forked. A florescent green line marked the way to the left. Albert's heart was pounding, his adrenaline rushing. He was finally back. He was back underground, back in the tunnels, back at the door to the temple. It was just ahead.

In the glow of the flashlights, a wall materialized.

"What the *fuck*?" Wayne spat, and Albert almost laughed. Thirteen months ago, Brandy spoke those same words in just about the exact same spot.

The man with no eyes must have reassembled the wall after they left last time, because he and Brandy certainly hadn't taken the time to do it.

"Relax," Albert said. He walked up to the wall, the déjà vu of the situation sending shivers of excitement through his skin, and placed the palm of his hand against the wall. For a moment he stood there, relishing the adventure he was about to get a second chance at. He closed his eyes, too excited, too thrilled to be at all anxious. Then, finally, he opened his eyes and pushed.

Chapter 5

For one horrible second Albert thought that he was wrong, that the wall at the end of the tunnel would not fall down, that the temple would not be there at all. The bricks hesitated for just that instant, taunting him, making him wonder if such unbelievable things could simply vanish as mysteriously as they were found, but then the bricks fell. The temple was there, just as it was the last time, just as it had always been.

The first room of the temple was just as Albert and Brandy last saw it. The five statues still stood in their respective places, their smooth, featureless faces staring at nothing and everything all at once. Like the first time they saw them, they were transfixed by the lifelike detail in these stone sentinels. They looked as though they could step away from the wall and reach out to them, not stone at all but flesh and blood.

“Unbelievable,” Nicole exclaimed, a hint of unmistakable ecstasy in her voice. She never doubted her friends’ story about the temple and the statues, but seeing them with her own eyes was an awesome experience nonetheless. She felt as though she had just glimpsed Atlantis or the Loch Ness Monster. Her eyes drifted down one of the statues to its enormous penis. “Look at the size of that guy’s cock!”

Wayne glanced at her, startled.

“Wait ‘til you see him with a full-blown hard-on,” said Brandy and then giggled as she saw the look on Wayne’s face.

Albert chuckled.

“What are they?” Wayne asked.

“We don’t know,” replied Albert.

“Jesus.” Wayne stepped up to one of them, studying it, impressed by its powerful presence. “The detail…” he awed. “It doesn’t look possible.”

“I can’t believe I’m seeing them,” Nicole sighed. She

touched one of them, ran her fingertips down its smooth, muscular chest to its hairless groin. She pulled her hand back for a moment, considering, and then she reached out again and touched its penis quickly, bashfully, as though to see if the faceless man might react.

"Okay," Albert announced. "Listen up. This place is dangerous. Some of these statues do things to you. They *affect* you."

"Affect us how?" Wayne asked.

"Lust, hate and fear."

Wayne turned and faced Albert. "Lust?"

Albert nodded, embarrassed. "You'll lose control. It's… Intense."

Wayne stared at him for a moment. He remembered Albert saying something to Nicole back in Gilbert House about a room full of statues that could make someone insanely horny, but he hadn't elaborated. While explaining it to him, he'd only described hate and fear. But he supposed he wouldn't have been eager to talk about something like that with a stranger.

After all that he'd already seen, he did not doubt that there were such rooms down here, but he had a hard time imagining that he could actually lose control just by entering one of them. “How?”

“Don’t know,” Brandy replied, as though plucking the two words right from Albert’s mouth.

Albert turned and shined his light into the left tunnel. He could still see the broken finger that marked the correct way, the only blemish on an otherwise perfect statue. Again, he wondered why someone would choose to deface such an impressive statue simply for the sake of giving him a clue. And why only this one? There had been no other broken statue pieces in the box. “Let’s go. We’ll all stick close together.”

Wayne walked up to the center statue and studied it, curiously observing its wild and erratic pose.

“It’s a warning,” Albert explained. “Without its face, you can’t tell what the pose means. At least that’s what I assume. He’s standing between the two passages.”

“What happens if we choose the wrong one?” Wayne asked. He eyed the two passages warily. Both were six feet lower than the floor of the chamber in which they stood, without the convenience of steps or a ramp. They would have to climb down to continue forward.

“Don’t ask.” Nicole wrapped her arms around herself as if cold.

Wayne glanced back at her and then turned again to Albert, who nodded agreement. “Okay. I won’t.”

“Come on,” Albert said. “Let’s get going.”

Albert dropped into the left passage and then turned and offered a hand to Brandy and then to Nicole. Wayne came last, not waiting for Albert’s kind hand. If he couldn’t drop six feet by himself he might as well just wait for them here.

When everyone was in the lower passage with him, Albert started forward. Ahead was the entrance to the sex room. He had no idea how the four of them were going to get through it, especially he and Brandy, who already knew what was in there. Last time they were here, they were unable to pass through it even with Brandy’s poor eyes blinding her to the statues. He had only barely managed to drag her back into this entrance chamber before succumbing to the room’s strange, sexual power.

“Oh my god.” Nicole gasped as she entered the room. She had imagined this chamber so many times, but her wildest dreams were not as fantastic as the reality of this place. Their flashlights did not nearly reach to its far end. On either side, the statues were lined up against the wall, ready as always to act out their silent message.

"It's another warning." Albert walked forward, shining his light on the statues along one of the walls. "As you look from one to the next, they change slightly, like frames in a cartoon."

Wayne followed after him, studying the statues as they appeared, one-by-one, from the looming darkness before them. "They're getting…um…"

"Yeah," Albert said. "It's the sex room. It's just ahead. We won't be able to look at the statues in there."

"Are they the same as these?"

Albert shook his head. "No. They're different."

Wayne stared at each new statue that appeared, hardly able to believe what he was seeing. Each one was slightly more aroused than the last, its penis slightly more erect. Soon they stood fully engorged and jutting toward the ceiling. It was absurdly vulgar, and yet he found it difficult to tear his eyes away from those enormous appendages. "Do the ones in there have faces?"

"Yeah. They're pornographic. They could be real

people turned to stone."

"Wow. And just looking at them makes you horny?"

"Out of control horny," Brandy confirmed, and instantly began to blush.

"Yeah. Look." Albert turned his flashlight straight ahead as they approached the far wall. Out of the darkness, the door to the sex room was appearing. The woman's face was intense, the expression frozen in such severe lust that it almost hurt the mind to look upon it.

"My god," was all that Wayne could think to say.

Nicole stepped up beside them, her eyes wide. "It's unbelievable."

"She's…I don't even know," said Wayne. "I couldn't even begin."

The four of them shined their flashlights onto the face. Even Albert felt his breath taken away, as though he were looking upon her for the first time.

"How do we get through?" Brandy asked. She could not take her eyes off the stone woman's mouth, the black opening that was the doorway into the sex room. She remembered the first time they went in there, remembered the statues that were in that room, that were *still* in that room today. She remembered what she and Albert did in there, the power of it, the *intensity* of it. She often remembered their experience in there, often thought of it when they were making love, and it always turned her on. Looking at the woman's face, she realized with sick dread that she was *already* turned on. Unwanted warmth began to radiate from deep in her belly. It was like an overwhelming urge to do something bad, the way recovering alcoholics must feel when they want to take a drink.

"How'd you get through the first time?" Wayne asked.

"We didn't," Albert replied.

"Brandy's glasses," Nicole said. "She can't see without them so she can get us through. That's how they did it before. We can do it again."

Albert shook his head. "Didn't work on the way out." He looked at Brandy and saw the distress on her face. It wouldn't work this time, either. He already knew this much.

"It's been over a year," Nicole said. "It couldn't happen again, could it?"

"I'll bet it could." Albert turned his eyes to the woman's face. That same, sick warmth was burning in his belly as well. He felt a mild sort of loathing for himself as he realized that the crotch of his jeans was suddenly not quite roomy enough.

"Hey, guys." Wayne turned off his flashlight. He was no longer looking at the face. He was looking back the way they came. "Kill your lights."

Albert hesitated, exchanged a curious look with the girls and then did as Wayne said and turned off his flashlight. Brandy and Nicole did the same. Blackness swallowed them and for a moment Albert wondered what their new friend was up to. But then he saw. Not all was black, as he'd first perceived. A dim glow was radiating from behind them, far up the tunnel through which the four of them had just traveled. Albert had just a moment to wonder who or what was back there before he realized that Wayne was no longer beside them. He was a dark shape moving swiftly toward the other end of the room.

"What's going on?" Nicole whispered.

Albert could hear the nervousness in her voice and did not blame her. "Come on. Get out of sight."

As the three of them crowded into the sex room door, Wayne made his way to the far wall and pressed his back against it. For what seemed like ages to his pounding heart, he waited beside the tunnel's entrance. The light grew steadily stronger and brighter, the intruder obviously cautious, but still in a hurry.

Wayne glanced forward again, toward where Albert and the girls were hiding, but he could see nothing but darkness. With the exception of the approaching light, it was utterly black.

He couldn't imagine who could have followed them down here. Had they attracted the attention of the police? He knew the steam tunnels were forbidden to students, but if they hadn't been close enough to catch them before they descended below the steam tunnels, what chance would anyone have of catching them all the way down here? And a malicious presence would almost certainly be more careful than whoever this was.

Finally, the source of the light came into view. It was a small flashlight, the kind one might keep in the glove box of a car in case of an emergency. An arm followed it and in the space of a heartbeat, the intruder was in sight and stepping into the room.

Wayne lunged, and even as he grabbed the intruder's arms, yanking them painfully back, he recognized her.

Beverly Bridger shrieked as much in horror as in pain as Wayne lifted her off her feet. Her flashlight tumbled to the floor and winked out, swallowing them both in perfect darkness. But this darkness was short lived. Three more flashlights came to life and bore down on her from the other side of the room.

"*LET GO OF ME*!"

"You stubborn, thick-headed, ballsy *bitch*!" Wayne spat. He couldn't believe this woman. The sheer nerve of her coming down here filled him with absolute rage. Was she stupid as well as crazy?

"*YOU PUT ME DOWN*!" She began to kick wildly and when one of her heels struck his shin, he did exactly as she demanded, hurling her forward and away from him. She sprawled onto the stone floor and let out a painful yelp.

"I don't fucking believe it!" Nicole said as she, Albert and Brandy approached the pathetic figure on the floor.

"That stupid bitch," Brandy agreed. Although Beverly seemed to be in pain, she was far too astounded by the woman's audacity to truly care. Obviously, Wayne had been in an agitated and emotional state when he came out of Gilbert House. What did she think he would do when he caught her following them?

"If you ask me," Nicole continued, "we should just let Wayne kill her. That seems to be what she wants." The words were not true, of course. She would never abide anyone physically harming another person, but she couldn't help but marvel over this woman's nerve.

Albert said no such thing, although he wondered if that wasn't the case. Her unrelenting persistence was astounding. He wanted to ask her if she was really this stupid. What he said to her instead was simply, "Are you all right?"

Beverly said nothing. She was curled up on her side, her eyes closed, her face pressed against the cold floor, softly sobbing.

Albert knelt beside her and observed the situation. She had not even bothered to change before following them into the tunnels. She was still wearing the black shirt from which Wayne had ripped the buttons. It was held closed by a knot at her belly and Albert found it amazing that Wayne's angry roughness had not pulled it apart to again reveal the woman's plain white bra, most of which remained clearly visible even with it tied. He could still see the scratch on her cheek from when Wayne threw her into the bushes outside Gilbert House, a shallow but rough gouge that he was sure still hurt. But this scratch did not seem to be the cause of her suffering. She was holding her left wrist, the same one she'd been holding to her bosom when they left her sprawled on the forest floor.

He reached for her arm, meaning to look at it, to see if it was sprained or even broken, but as he was leaning over her, she opened her eyes. What he saw in them was pure and utter terror.

"*DON'T YOU TOUCH ME*!" she screamed, startling them all. Her voice was shrill, like that of a young child who has become convinced that the boogeyman just wrapped its cold claws around her ankle. She scrambled away from Albert and right back to where Wayne stood frozen with astonishment. "*LEAVE ME ALONE*!" Her voice echoed through the empty chamber as she began to claw at his jeans. "*DON'T YOU LET HIM TOUCH ME*!"

Albert looked at Wayne, his eyes wide and startled, and Wayne returned the look. The woman was insane. She had to be.

She pulled herself up to her knees using Wayne's pant leg as a handhold, and then actually *clung* to him. As she did this she opened her mouth and let out a long, wailing cry, one part scream, one part sob, in an odd sort of melodrama that was eerily frightening.

Nicole clapped her hands over her ears.

Wayne was too surprised to do more than gape at her.

As Albert got back to his feet, Brandy pushed her body against his as though to comfort herself from this woman's insane fit. "What's wrong with her?"

Albert shook his head. "I have no idea."

For what seemed like a long time, Beverly clung to Wayne's leg, sobbing in great, wet heaves. Wayne stood where he was, uncomfortable as hell, but almost afraid to move. Albert, Brandy and Nicole all stood where they were, watching with a horrified sort of fascination this woman who'd had not only the courage but also the audacity to follow them into the Temple of the Blind, and then bawled like a terrified child when Albert tried to help her.

When she finally let go of Wayne's leg and allowed him to step away from her, Brandy cautiously approached her. "Are you okay?" she asked.

The woman looked up at her, her dark eyes wet and rimmed with red. She did not speak, but she did not shrink away, either. Apparently, it was only Albert who frightened her.

Brandy knelt before the woman and cautiously reached out to her.

Beverly did not stop her from taking the hand she held against her bosom, but she kept her eyes locked on Albert.

"Is it broken?" Brandy asked.

Beverly did not look at her. "I don't know," she whispered.

"Does it hurt bad?"

She shook her head. "Better now."

"Can you move it?"

Beverly moved her wrist back and forth slowly, wincing a little as she did it. Brandy could see that it was swollen.

"I think it's sprained. But I'm no doctor."

"Maybe she should see one," Wayne said, not really meaning the guy in the X-ray room.

Beverly shook her head. "I'm fine." But the quiver in her voice suggested otherwise.

"What are you doing down here?" Nicole asked.

For a moment, it seemed that she was not going to answer, but then she softly replied, "I…didn't get…what I needed…"

"Beverly," Albert said, and although he came no closer to her, she cringed as though he had slapped her, "when we were in Gilbert House, Wayne found a girl hiding in the bathroom. She'd been there since Wednesday night, since *you* sent her in there. She had no food. She had nothing to drink." The woman's eyes grew a little, perhaps with regret or remorse, but he could not tell for certain. "That girl's dead now, dragged off into some kind of dark forest. Does that mean anything to you?"

Beverly lowered her eyes to the floor, not wanting to meet his powerful gaze.

"It means a lot to Wayne, here. That's why he did what he did to you earlier. I can't blame him, honestly. Can you?"

Still, she said nothing. Though she looked twice their age, she resembled a scolded child on the verge of more tears.

"Albert," Brandy said, urging him to stop.

"I just want to know why. Why follow us down here? You knew he would probably hurt you again. Why send us in there to begin with? Why the obsession with Gilbert House?"

"I can't..." Beverly began, her voice barely audible. "I can't go in."

"What?"

"I can't go inside Gilbert House," Beverly said, louder this time. "It's like...like a bonfire. I can only get so close and then..."

"What?" Albert pushed. "It burns you?"

Beverly nodded miserably. "Yes. Sort of."

"And you still have to know what's in it?" Nicole

asked, doubtful.

"It lures me," Beverly explained. "It calls to me. I don't know how. I don't know why."

Albert was at last beginning to understand the situation a little bit.

"Look, I'm sorry those kids are dead, okay! I didn't want that to happen. I…just wanted to know what was in there…why it calls to me." She paused, her expression wretched, she was still staring at the floor, still cradling her sore wrist to her bosom. "It's making me crazy."

"No shit," muttered Nicole.

"All we saw," Albert explained, "was that Gilbert House is completely built on the inside and that when you look through the windows all you can see is a dark forest."

"Yeah," Wayne added. "That and a five-hundred-pound midget on steroids."

"That thing almost killed them both," Nicole said, less explaining to Beverly than reflecting on how close she and Brandy had come to losing Albert. "It had them. It would have killed them if something bigger hadn't come along and…" A violent shudder prevented her from finishing.

"Whatever took Olivia was bad enough to scare the shit out of that thing," Brandy said. "It would've gotten me if I'd been closer to the window than—"

"Stop," Wayne pleaded.

For a long moment, the five of them were silent but for the sounds of Beverly's wet sniffles.

"That's all we can tell you," Albert said at last. "Go back up, get a new shirt on and go get that wrist checked out."

Beverly shook her head. "I want to come with you."

"*Absolutely not*," Wayne said so quickly that Beverly flinched.

Albert agreed with him. "It's dangerous up ahead. You're in no condition to—"

"I can feel it!" she said, turning her wide, dark eyes on Albert again. Her sudden burst of energy startled him. There was an intensity in those eyes that made him want to take a step backward.

"What?"

"What I felt in Gilbert House…that thing that calls to me…I feel it down here, too."

Albert stared at her, not sure what her words meant.

"I don't know why I came down here. I guess I thought I could just follow and listen, maybe find out what you saw, but when I got closer, I started to feel it. It's that luring I felt from Gilbert House, but without the…the burning."

Albert considered this for a moment, not sure what he should do.

"Do you think she can make it?" Nicole asked.

Albert shook his head. "I don't know. We can try."

"No way!" Wayne insisted. "She's nuts. Dangerous. I don't trust her."

Albert ignored him. He looked at Beverly and said, "That's the sex room up there. If you open your eyes in there you won't be able to control yourself."

She nodded. "I know."

Albert remembered her saying that she dreamt about him and Brandy in the temple and he found the idea more than a little disturbing.

"You're not really considering this, are you?" Wayne demanded.

Albert turned his eyes on him. He didn't speak, but

the weight of his eyes silenced him. “This goes for everyone here. I think it would be very dangerous to get stuck in there.” He looked down at Beverly, fixing her with his gaze. He did not want to frighten or upset her, but he needed to make sure that she knew what she’d be getting herself into. “If you went in by yourself,” he explained, “you wouldn’t have the willpower to come back out. You’d probably masturbate first, but that wouldn’t be enough. You’d start begging for someone to come help you. At first you might prefer a member of the opposite sex, but it really wouldn’t matter. Anyone would do. You wouldn’t care.”

Beverly stared back at him, her eyes wide and clear. The others were also staring at him.

“Eventually, I think you’d try to do the statues. I don’t think finding one with an accessible erection would be a problem. You’d just pick one. You wouldn’t even care that your uterus ruptures because in there, all you care about is satisfying urges you don’t want and can’t control. In there, you don’t care about anything but the sex. You don’t care about the pain. You don’t even care about the orgasms. You only want more, maybe right up until you bleed to death."

For a moment there was complete silence in the room, and then Albert asked Beverly, "Do you still want to go?"

Beverly nodded. "I have to," she said.

"But now I don't know if *I* want to go," Wayne muttered.

Albert did not seem to hear. "If anyone wants to turn back, now's the time to do it."

Nobody spoke. Nobody was out.

"Okay, then. Let's get going." Albert turned and walked across the room, between the rows of sentinels that so vulgarly saluted him, chasing away the shadows with his flashlight.

Beverly let the others go first and then picked up her flashlight and examined it. A small shake got it glowing again and with the light came a little relief. The batteries probably weren't the freshest and she did not want to be stuck down here relying on other people's flashlights.

Albert paused in front of the sex room door and stared at the woman's face, pondering.

"I can't," said Brandy as she and Nicole stepped up

beside him. “I won’t make it.” She looked from Albert to Nicole, pleading for understanding. She had been afraid to go in there before, but after Albert’s speech, she could hardly bear the thought of it.

“Yeah,” Albert said. He looked at Nicole. “You don’t wear contacts, do you?”

Nicole shook her head.

“How about you, Wayne? Do you wear contacts?”

Wayne was still walking toward them, his gaze fixed on the statues he was passing. “Yeah, actually.”

“You may have to lead us through the first room.”

“Why can’t Brandy?”

“Because she and I know what’s in there. What little she can see without her glasses is just enough to remember what we saw the first time. I don’t know if the intensity would be the same, but she still may not be able to control herself.”

Wayne nodded, understanding the situation. “But hey, instead of me taking out my contacts, which I really don’t want to lose,” he said, looking at Brandy, “why don’t you lend someone else your glasses. Then they’d see what you see when you take yours off.”

"Hey, that's true," said Nicole.

Albert looked at Brandy. He had never considered that. "That might work."

Beverly was walking warily toward them, her eyes fixed on Albert as though he might suddenly turn and lunge at her.

"So who gets the glasses?" Brandy asked.

Albert looked from Nicole to Wayne and back again. "I might be able to do it. But I don't know that for sure."

"I'll take them," said Nicole. It was hard to mistake the eagerness in her voice. She'd been fascinated by the idea of the temple, and particularly this room, ever since Albert and Brandy first told her the story.

"And if you start to feel weird at all," said Wayne. "You can pass them right to me."

"That's true," Brandy said. "We could go in shifts."

Albert's expression lit up. "That could get us through the fear room!"

"Okay!" Nicole held her hand out to Brandy. "Give me your glasses and let's go!"

Chapter 6

As she stepped into the moaning woman's mouth, Nicole felt an odd sort of anxiety. Through her best friend's glasses, the world around her was shallow and featureless, like the faces on the statues. Those around her were reduced to human shapes and colors and the Temple of the Blind became nothing more than shades of gray fading into black. Ahead of her, in the throat of the woman upon whose stone tongue she now tread, there was only thick darkness. It was this darkness that made her heart beat faster with anxious anticipation.

"Remember," Albert said, "no matter how tempting it is, don't look around the glasses."

"Okay." But she already knew that this would be

easier said than done. Brandy's glasses were small and stylish, with narrow, rectangular lenses. She would have to peer straight ahead at all times, and remember to always turn her head and not her eyes. It would prove difficult if she became scared. Simple reflexes made her want to glance out the corners of her eyes or peer over the top to make sure there was nothing hiding in the shadows around her.

She stepped into the room and tried to focus on the things directly in front of her, on a path that would lead her and her friends through this insane room and to the other side safely. Directly in front of her, on the floor, the first of the sex room's statues appeared from the gloom. She could see the outline of a person sprawled before her, but so far the lust-inducing details were lost. All that she could discern from this statue was that it was in the shape of a human, a woman, she thought.

Albert and Brandy described some of the statues they saw in this room on one occasion and Nicole, while unaffected by their mere descriptions, was amazed at how uncomfortable they both became. They were unable to sit still and she had even observed with considerable embarrassment the noticeable bulge in the crotch of Albert's shorts. Even after all that time, the sex room still affected them, the very memory of it strong enough to ignite their lust.

As wrong as it was, she wanted to see it. She wanted to look upon the statues in this room, to see what could make a person do such things without care of consequences, even against his or her own personal principles. She ached to see it, to know that impossible feeling, but she resisted these dangerous urges. She tore her eyes from the statue at her feet and took a deep breath. "Where do I go?" she asked.

"The door's straight ahead," Albert replied. "You just have to make your way around the statues."

"Okay." Nicole took another deep breath, still resisting the urge to take just a little peek. "Is everyone ready?"

She felt Brandy's hand grasp the back belt loop of her jeans. "We're ready."

"Everyone stay close." She took one last deep, relaxing breath and began to walk.

All around her, things jutted out at her. Hands and

feet and elbows and heads seemed to come from impossible angles. Things came and went before her eyes, emerging from the gloom and then fading back into it again. Some even passed close enough for her to discern considerable detail, but they were only there for a moment.

"You guys said you saw what was in here the first time?" Wayne asked. He was behind Albert, one hand grasping his cotton tee shirt, the other still brandishing his flashlight. Behind him, Beverly was taking up the rear. He had wanted her to go first, not really trusting his back to her, but she refused to go near Albert.

"Yeah," Albert replied. "We didn't know."

"How did you get out?"

"Someone came while we were...*occupied*...and took our flashlight. When the light faded, so did the urges."

"Who took the light?"

"The man with no eyes, I guess."

The man with no eyes? Wayne found the concept impossible, but he had no reason to doubt their word. "So you really would have just kept doing it? Until...what?

Until your hearts burst?"

"I think so. Until *something* happened."

"Unbelievable."

"Is it a bad thing?" Nicole asked. "Having seen what's in here?" To her right, she could make out the shape of a man who appeared to be taking a woman from behind, and she felt something. She wondered if that was just her imagination or if she had actually felt a tiny bit of the sex room's strange power. Or perhaps it was just her natural reaction to that particular sexual position. It was rather naughty, after all.

"I think it can be," Albert replied.

"It isn't for us," said Brandy. "Not really."

"It's sort of good for us, I think," agreed Albert. "We have each other. We share it. But I don't know how it would be for someone else."

Nicole considered this. She wondered what it would be like for someone like her, someone who didn't have someone wonderful to share it with. Would the memory of a room like this only give her yearnings that she could never hope to satisfy? Would it change her? Would it turn her into something bad, into some kind of shameless sex addict? Would she become some nasty slut begging strangers on the street for cheap sex? She supposed it was possible. She would be a sexually driven creature with no outlet for her urges, whereas Albert and Brandy would always have each other.

The thought was enough to strengthen her resolve to not peek at the statues. And yet, even with strengthened resolve, the statues kept taunting her from her peripheral vision, outside the protective lenses of Brandy's glasses.

"How are we doing?" Wayne asked. "Are we almost there?"

"I'm not sure," Nicole confessed. "I think so."

A woman appeared in the flashlight's beam directly ahead of her. She was up high, sitting on a man's shoulders and therefore positioned above the glasses. She was facing the man she was riding, clutching his hair in both hands and forcing her crotch into his face. He was likewise groping her buttocks, pulling her against him. The sight took her by surprise and without thinking she lowered her face and saw that there was another woman on her knees in front of the man, her face buried against his groin as another man seized her from behind.

She closed her eyes and forced the image from her mind. She could absolutely feel it now, that deep aching. She was nowhere near losing control. She still had no desire to turn around and attack Albert or Wayne, but she could almost see how it could escalate out of control. That was only one statue. What if she removed Brandy's glasses and gazed openly at the entire room?

"How's everybody feeling?" Albert asked. "Nicole?"

"I'm all right," she replied. And she *was* all right. She did suddenly feel a little uncomfortable between her legs, but the very fact that she was not about to admit that to her best friend's boyfriend was proof enough that she still maintained control.

She wondered if it was possible that Albert and Brandy could have fallen victim to this room more easily because of their particular situation. After all, they were both single that night and already attracted to each other even before they came down here. They'd both admitted as much to her.

Her eyes were drawn to a figure on her right and she caught a glimpse past the glasses of a gray man gripping his swollen penis with one hand as he reached for something with the other. Immediately she forced her attention forward again as that strange yearning swelled deep in her gut. The sight of the man's penis remained at the center of her thoughts like some lingering odor and her fear of this room grew a little. How little would it take?

"How are the glasses working?" Albert asked.

"They're okay. A little easier to peek around than I'd like, but I'm still okay."

"You sure?"

"Yeah."

"You can switch with Wayne if it gets too bad."

"I said I'm not horny. God, Brandy, tell your boyfriend it's just not going to happen."

Brandy laughed. "Oh, he *knows*!"

Albert chuckled. "Okay, okay. I'm just making sure you're all right."

"I am. I promise."

"That's good," Albert said. "Brandy?"

"I'm hanging in there."

"Are you going to be okay?" he pressed.

"Yeah. I'm fine. Don't worry." And she was. She

was in no danger of falling into this trap again. She didn't feel that endless desire that had made her turn and throw herself at Albert the last time she was in here, but the memory of this place alone was enough to fill her with primal wanting. Even with her eyes closed, she could feel her body reacting to what she knew surrounded her.

"Okay," Albert said, trusting her. "Wayne?"

"No sweat."

"Good. Beverly?"

There was no reply.

"Beverly?" Albert felt a tinge of unease creeping up his spine.

Wayne could feel her right behind him. She had grasped his shirt exactly as he had grasped Albert's before they entered this room.

"I can see it," Beverly whispered hoarsely.

"What?" Brandy asked, startled.

"Close your damn eyes!" Wayne demanded.

"They *are* closed!" Beverly nearly screamed. "I don't see it with my eyes! I see it with my *mind*!"

"How?" Albert asked. The five of them had now stopped. Their full attention was now focused upon the sound of Beverly's quickening breath.

Beverly did not reply, perhaps *could* not reply. She groaned sickly, almost moaned. She was going to lose control.

"Come on, guys!" Albert gave Brandy a gentle nudge to pass to Nicole. "We need to be moving!"

Nicole continued her blind trek through the sex room, slowly maneuvering around the complex tangle of stone body parts that stood between them and the exit. As the sound of Beverly's heavy breathing intensified behind her, she lost any urge to see more of the things around her. In fact, she began to grow afraid. She wanted out. She lifted her chin up and peered down through the glasses, eliminating the ability to peek over them. "How will I know the way out?"

"It's a square opening in the wall," Albert said. He managed to sound calm, but he was quickly becoming frantic. If Beverly lost control in this room, he could not guarantee that one or more of them would not get separated, turned around and lost.

Wayne stuffed his flashlight into the waistband of his pants and then reached back and gripped Beverly's wrist hard enough to hurt her. Had it been her bad wrist, the pain might have been intense enough to make some difference, but she was holding onto him with her right hand, still keeping the left one close to her chest, her flashlight pressed uselessly against her breast. A silent rage was boiling up within him, driving his fingers into her flesh. He did not like Beverly Bridger. He did not trust her. She was going to be trouble for them, he was certain. And God help him, if she got anybody hurt down here he would make her pay. He might even kill her.

Up ahead, Nicole shouted, "I think I see it!" Before her, in the midst of a tangle of formless gray, a dark opening appeared.

"Thank God!" Brandy sighed. With her eyes firmly closed, she was still thankfully in complete control of herself (if more than a little uncomfortable) but she was intensely relieved to be out of harm's way if only for Beverly's sake.

Nicole stepped through the doorway and into the small chamber that waited beyond it. As she slipped Brandy's glasses off her face, the others exited behind her.

Wayne stepped through the opening behind Albert and, still gripping her wrist, jerked Beverly out of the sex room hard enough that she stumbled and fell to the floor.

"Wayne, that's *enough*!" Brandy scolded. It was one thing to be angry, but there was no reason for this sort of roughness.

"I'm sorry!" Wayne said, his voice still sharp with anger. "But what the *fuck* was that?"

"*I'm sorry*!" Beverly cried, nearly weeping. "*I didn't know*!"

"Yeah. Just like you didn't know the people you were sending into Gilbert House were probably going to get their brains squeezed out?"

"Wayne, don't," Albert pleaded.

Beverly began to sob. "*I didn't choose this*!" she wept. "*I never wanted to be this way*!"

"What way?" Nicole asked.

"Psychic," Albert answered for her.

Beverly nodded miserably.

Brandy and Nicole looked at each other, surprised.

"That's how she saw us down here the first time. In her dream."

She looked up at him through her tears, surprised. "Yeah."

"And someone like her would probably feel Gilbert House from miles away."

Beverly nodded.

"Probably because of that forest. Gilbert House stands in a different world."

She looked up at him, considering. Yes, that could be it. That would make perfect sense. If Gilbert House stood in a different world and acted as a gateway to that place, then perhaps it was something on the other side that was calling to her. She was not being drawn *to* Gilbert House but *through* it, yet she was unable to approach it for some reason. That might also explain why she felt the same pull so strongly down here. This place might be connected to that same world.

"If you ask me," Wayne said, seemingly uninterested in the conversation at hand, "we should just leave her."

"How can you say that?" Brandy asked, actually appalled by his lack of sympathy.

"He may be right," Albert said.

Brandy and Nicole looked at him, surprised.

“She almost didn’t make it through the sex room. What if she doesn’t get through the hate room?”

No one offered a reply to this question. The hate room was more dangerous than the sex room and not merely because of the spiked pit at its far end. If she, or any of them for that matter, were to be affected by the statues in the hate room, the rest of them would be in danger.

“But we can’t just leave her,” Brandy said.

Beverly stared at them, her wet eyes now wide and afraid. She did not want to be left alone in this place. She had nowhere to go but back and she would not be able to get through the sex room a second time.

“Well, she doesn’t have to stay here,” Albert decided. “The hate room’s a long ways ahead.”

Brandy nodded, at least temporarily satisfied. “Okay. Let’s get going.”

Chapter 7

"How long is this maze?" Nicole asked. She remembered Albert and Brandy telling her that the first time they came here they'd been forced to continue from the sex room without their clothes. She could hardly imagine treading these cold, stone corridors barefoot, much less stark naked.

"I don't remember exactly," Albert replied. He had wondered for a moment if he'd be able to remember the way. He did not mark it the first time he came through because he'd lost the paint can along with his backpack, but as he walked, he found that the path was burned perfectly into his memory. It was as though he'd only been here yesterday. "If I remember right, this last passage was pretty long."

"Just as long as we don't get lost," Nicole replied.

"I don't think so," Brandy said. "This feels right to me. I'm more worried about what we're going to do when we get to the hate room."

"I know," said Albert. It seemed to be true that those rooms relied on vision in order to affect people. Brandy had been able to navigate the hate room safely without her glasses, both on the way in and on the way out. And for a time it had even worked in the fear room, until her fear got the better of her. But the trick failed her in the sex room, where she'd already been exposed to the perverse statues on her way in. But by using Brandy's glasses to encumber her own vision, Nicole had been able to navigate the sex room much as Brandy had done the hate room. That told him that the trick ought to work for any one of them, assuming they weren't already familiar with the statues in the room he or she was attempting to navigate. But Beverly's psychic abilities apparently allowed her to see the room even with her eyes tightly shut.

He wondered how her abilities worked. What was it,

exactly, that had allowed her to see the sex room? "Beverly," he inquired, "when you said you dreamed about us coming down here last year, what exactly did you see?"

For a moment, he wasn't sure she was going to allow him a reply, but she did. "It was…only half a dream, I think," she explained. "When I saw you go in, I'm sure I was dreaming, but by the time you came out, I was wide awake in bed, staring up at my ceiling, but also directly at you. I saw you like I was there with you."

"I see. What did you feel when we went into the sex room?"

"I…I saw you having sex in there," she said bluntly.

Brandy's breath caught in her throat. The thought that this woman—or anyone, for that matter—had seen them down here at that precise moment, when they both had lost control and given into unjustified lust, was mortifying. She had felt pity for her, but at that moment she felt violated. At that moment, she almost *hated* Beverly Bridger.

"I was turned on," Beverly went on, a little embarrassed, "but not by the room, I don't think. I was more turned on by the two of you, the furious passion of it all, by the suddenness of it. It was so...*unexpected*."

Albert nodded. He was neither mortified nor angry. His interest did not lie there, but in more important matters. "Could you see the room? Could you see the statues?"

She considered this for a moment and then shook her head. "I don't remember exactly, but I think so. I'm pretty sure. When I was in there just now, I could remember the statues from my dream. It was like I knew everything that was around me. I didn't have to see it."

Again Albert nodded. It was similar to how Brandy had remembered the sex room when they passed through it the second time. She fell victim to the lust again simply because she could remember it from the first time. "And what about the hate room? Did you see it?"

Beverly opened her mouth to reply, but then closed it again. She had been about to say yes, of course she had seen it, just as she had seen the sex room before it and the fear room after it, but that was not quite true. "I don't know," she confessed instead. "I feel like I did. I saw *you* in there, but..." She shook her head. "But I don't remember seeing the statues…or *any* of that room for that matter. It's like…it was dark or something."

Again he nodded. "Is it possible that you saw the temple *through* us? *Only* through us?"

Beverly considered this. "Yes. That's possible. It's likely, actually."

"Because *we* saw the sex room. But we never saw the hate room. Brandy wasn't wearing her glasses. If your vision was based entirely on ours, then you won't have any memory of the things in there."

"And she'll be able to cross the hate room!" Nicole exclaimed.

"You really think that'll work?" Wayne asked, doubtful.

"No, I don't," replied Albert. "It's just a theory. But we have to try. The only other option is to abandon her between the two rooms."

Wayne glanced back at Beverly as he imagined leaving her behind in these dark corridors, abandoning her the way she abandoned Olivia to her awful fate within Gilbert House. He saw her face pale with dread, and was a little surprised at the lack of satisfaction he felt. He still blamed her for what became of Olivia and her friends. He still hated her for what she did. He would never trust her. But neither could he be so cruel as to leave her behind in this cold darkness with no way out.

They turned the final corner in the passage and found the praying sentinel. This time, no one seemed startled by its appearance.

Albert paused and gazed upon it, remembering the last time, when he and Brandy were fresh from their intercourse, cold and naked. She was so beautiful, so angelic. A part of him almost wished they were like that again, alone and naked, intimate and vulnerable.

"Faith," he said, chasing the thoughts from his head. Without explaining himself to the others, he went on.

The other four followed, traveling ever deeper down the gentle slope. Along the way, something appeared on the path before them and Albert paused to stare at it. It was the green cap from the spray paint can they used to mark their way the first time they came down here. He remembered passing it on their way out without bothering to stop and pick it up. At the time, they were still desperate to put distance between themselves and that thing that chased them into the water. He took the time to gather the paint can, which was still at least half full, but the lid had seemed irrelevant at the time. Now, as he stared at it, the familiarity of the scene struck him with a chill.

"What is it?" Wayne asked.

"The lid from the spray paint can," Nicole replied. It was such a small detail, such a minor thing, but it was just another part of Albert and Brandy's amazing story that was unfolding before her eyes in brilliant reality. She could still scarcely believe she was actually here.

Brandy bent and picked it up. "It feels like ages, but it's like we dropped it here yesterday." She ran her fingers across it. "No dust."

"There doesn't seem to be any dust down here," Albert said. "It's amazingly clean."

"No cobwebs either," Wayne said.

"I know." Albert started walking again. He remembered Gilbert House and how it had been void of cobwebs, as though spiders and bugs were afraid to go inside. Could it be that bugs could feel what Beverly did when they approached Gilbert House? Could they feel the burning? But if that was true, then what kept them out of these tunnels?

Brandy lingered. She started to drop the lid, to just leave it where they found it, but somehow that seemed wrong. It was like littering. She removed her backpack instead and slipped it inside. There was no reason to leave it behind again.

Ahead of her, Albert stepped up to the water's edge and stopped. For a moment he stood and stared out over the still water, into the shadows beyond. On the other side was the round room with the dying sentinels. That room was where they found that creature last time. It came out of the darkness of one of the other tunnels and chased them. He never saw what it was. He hadn't dared take the time to look back. Not a day had gone by since that he hadn't wondered what that thing was. What was the peculiar noise it made? Why did it stop chasing them?

"We have to swim," he said when the others had gathered around him.

"What?" By the tone of Wayne's voice, one might think that he could not swim, but it was surprise rather than panic that gave an edge to his words.

“It’s going to be cold as hell,” Albert warned, “but we have to go.” He removed his backpack and unzipped it.

“I brought suits,” Brandy said. “But only for three of us.”

“I should have planned better,” Albert apologized. “I was in a hurry to get back down here. I should have stopped and made sure we had supplies for everybody. I wasn’t thinking.”

“Even if you had,” pointed out Nicole, “you couldn’t have known Beverly would be here.”

“That’s true,” Albert admitted. “But we could have bought some food and water to bring with us.” He shook his head. “I can’t believe I didn’t think about it. I’m better than this.”

“You were distracted over what happened in Gilbert House,” Brandy soothed. “We all were. We didn’t think about it either.”

Albert shook his head. He was smarter than this. The sodas and candy bars Brandy packed had been exactly what they needed when they found Olivia. That alone was reason enough to at least restock her backpack. But he had merely driven everyone straight here in his haste, not once even thinking.

He opened the box and removed Beverly's envelope from his bag. He intended to stuff it inside so that it would stay dry.

Beverly caught sight of the envelope and had to resist an urge to snatch it from his hand. "How did you get into my apartment?"

Albert looked at her. "What?"

"When you took that."

Albert looked down at the envelope. He remembered the accusation she made outside Gilbert House, that he had somehow stolen the envelope from her. She had even called him a liar when he told her about Andrea Prophett. "I told you how I got it." He looked up at her, curious. "You're really telling me that it wasn't you who gave it to that girl?"

"Why would I want you to have that?"

Albert stared at her, not understanding. "If you didn't want me to have it, why did you write my name and address on the front?" He held it up and showed it to her.

Beverly stared at the writing on the envelope. "I

didn't write that."

Albert turned it and stared at the writing. "But if you didn't…then who did?"

"It wasn't me," Beverly insisted. The tone of her voice was turning defensive. She truly seemed to believe that he was trying to deceive her.

But Albert wasn't listening to the venom in her voice. He was staring at the envelope, thinking. "If you didn't write it…" he said, his thoughts whirling inside his head. "That means somebody *else* knew we were down here."

Now Brandy was also staring at the envelope. "But who?"

Albert had no chance to answer. Behind him, Nicole shattered the empty silence of the temple with a startling scream. He twirled around, almost stumbling in his haste to see what was wrong.

For just an instant he did not see what had frightened her, but then he did and suddenly he felt a sick dread fill him as he realized that he knew nothing about these empty passages. All those months ago, he had stalked these tunnels so carefully, cautiously watching both his front and back, making assumptions and calculated judgments, but he was not so clever. He was a fool, in fact. He was stupid. He had looked back often, but how many times had he looked *up*?

It came not through the water but over it, clinging to the stone ceiling like a giant, pale spider, a swift, hairless thing scurrying toward them. For a moment its form remained a mystery, but then its shape caught up with the eye and Albert recognized it for what it was just before it dropped to the floor in front of them.

The five of them stood motionless, staring at the strange new arrival. Not one of them knew how to react.

The naked man seemed to stare back at them, yet it was physically impossible for him to see at all. Like the night Albert and Brandy first looked upon him, he had no eyes with which to see.

He took two deep sniffs of the air, as though he found their odor curious, and then immediately turned his eyeless face on Albert. He took two steps forward, closing to within an inch of Albert's face, and drew deeply of his scent. "You," he said, his voice hoarse and raw, as though his larynx were a rusty machine. He turned slightly and sniffed quickly three times in Brandy's direction. "And the woman."

Albert and Brandy exchanged an uncertain look.

The blind man took another deep inhalation of the air around him, slowly turning his head from left to right as he did so. He paused for a moment, as though considering the others who were there. He was facing Nicole, as if she was of particular interest, but then he turned his bald and eyeless face back to Albert. "Hurry." He stepped back, giving him room. "Remove your clothes."

"What?" Nicole sounded horrified.

"You must continue naked," the eyeless man explained. "Give me the ones closest to your skin. Leave the rest where you stand."

"No way!" Wayne felt suddenly trapped. A rush of anger toward this blind freak boiled up from deep inside.

"Why do you need our clothes?" Brandy asked.

"The clothes smell," the blind man said simply. "Leave them and bathe in the water or the hounds will smell."

"The hounds?" Albert felt overwhelmed.

"Hurry now!"

Nobody moved. Albert stared at the blind man for a moment, puzzled. Could he really be serious? “Are the hounds those things we heard last time? The things that make that noise?”

“Yes,” replied the blind man. “They are deaf and blind but they smell.”

“I see. And our underwear? The clothes closest to our skin?”

“I will take them ahead, to draw the hounds away.”

Now Albert understood. This was why their clothes had been stolen the first time, why their underwear had been hung in that strange maze.

“Hold on,” said Wayne. He felt overwhelmed. Hounds? This was the first he’d heard of such creatures. “This doesn’t make any sense. If those…whatever they are…have such a good sense of smell, then how are we going to be safe just by being naked? They won’t just be able to smell our clothes. We smell too.”

Albert nodded. This was exactly what he was thinking. “That’s right,” he said. “Why can’t we just give you what you need to take ahead and put the rest back on?”

“It is the way it must be done,” said the blind man. “Go forward without your clothes or turn back now.” The tone of his voice told them he had no patience for further protests.

“Is there more we should know?” pushed Albert. “Something that’ll help us understand why we have to leave our clothes here?”

“No. Now hurry.”

“I’m not taking my clothes off,” insisted Nicole. “I came to see the Temple of the Blind, not to be on *Girls Gone Wild*.”

“It’s unreasonable,” agreed Wayne. “There’s no sense in it.”

Brandy turned to Albert, her eyes pleading with him to say more, to convince the eyeless stranger that he couldn’t expect them to do this.

“I’ve said how it will be,” the blind man said. “You may take your bags and that is all. If you do not agree, then turn back now and never return.”

Wayne opened his mouth to say more, but the blind man cut him off.

“I will discuss it no more.”

Albert glanced back at the others, saw the expressions they wore and then looked back at the blind man. It didn't make sense. By allowing them to take their bags, this stranger had completely undermined his original argument. If the scent of the clothes would attract the hounds and not their bodies, then his backpack would be no different from his jeans. But then again, it was this man, he was sure, who got them in and out of the temple the first time. He glanced back up into the darkness behind them. There was a statue back there. Faith. Faith in the sentinels. Faith in the temple. Faith in whatever was down here. He looked back at the blind man and knew what he had to do. "I'm going," he said. He bent and untied his shoes. "Anyone who wants to turn back, go ahead. It should be pretty safe going the other way, just follow the marks on the walls.

Brandy stared at him. He couldn't be serious. She wanted to urge him to stay, but she knew he wouldn't.

"Me too," said Beverly.

Nicole looked at her and then at Wayne. This wasn't a part of the story. Albert and Brandy lost their clothes when they got stuck in the sex room. Albert had told her he suspected it was the blind man's way of urging them forward. But they knew the way now. They'd conquered the sex room. It wasn't fair that he take their clothes this time.

Wayne turned and looked back up the path behind them. He could find the way back. It wouldn't be hard. The tunnels were marked. The maze was small. He thought he could remember the turns. He could probably even feel his way through the sex room if he just kept his eyes closed and took his time. But then what? What would he do when he finally got home? He turned and looked back at the others. Beverly wasn't budging. She had little choice but to go. And Albert had already made up his mind. He was already taking off his shirt. That only left Brandy and Nicole. He wished like hell he knew what they were thinking. If either of them refused, he could return with her. He could make sure she was safe as they made their way back to the campus. He wouldn't even have to feel guilty for leaving.

As Albert unbuttoned his jeans, Brandy grunted and peeled off her shirt. She did not like this. Taking off her clothes again was bad enough. Doing it in front of everybody was countless times worse. But Albert was going to go. He was determined. Knowing the dangers ahead, he would gladly go without her, but she couldn't allow that. She came here to find an end to this nightmare, and she'd be damned if she was going to let him go on alone. The very thought of sitting down in her empty apartment and just waiting for him to come home, never really sure if he would even make it back… It would drive her insane.

Behind them, without hesitating, Beverly untied her shirt and dropped it. In almost the same motion, she reached behind her and unfastened her bra. This was a choice that had already been made for her. For decades something had been beckoning her. She would not be turned away now, not for the sake of something as trivial as her modesty.

Nicole watched, embarrassed, as her companions undressed. She couldn't believe they were really going to do this. It was absurd. This eyeless man wouldn't even give them a good reason. She caught Wayne's eye, saw that he, too, was hesitating. If she refused, he would turn back with her. She was sure of that. But that would mean leaving Albert and Brandy to go on alone. And what if she let them go on without her? Then what? Reluctantly, she unfastened her pants and pushed them down. She could not believe that she was doing this, but if her friends were willing, then so was she. She could not abandon them. If she turned back now, she would regret it for the rest of her life. And what if they needed her? She couldn't bear the thought of something happening to them because she refused to strip.

For a moment, Wayne watched as Brandy and Nicole stripped off their shirts and pants and bras. He did not come down here to go skinny-dipping, but he also did not come this far just to turn back because he did not want anyone to see his junk. With a grimace, he pulled off his shirt and gave in to the blind man's unreasonable request.

Seconds later, the five of them stood naked and embarrassed. Brandy gathered everyone's socks and underwear, noticing the interesting variety of styles from Wayne's boxers to Albert's briefs and from Beverly's practical, cotton panties to her own little pink thong that she wore just for Albert. When she had all of them, she turned and put them in the blind man's outstretched hand.

"The hounds are fast," the blind man warned, "but they cannot jump. Stay on the path or you'll be in the maze. Do not forget to use the box." This said, the blind man leapt to the ceiling and scurried away like a huge, pale insect, vanishing into the darkness as quickly as he'd appeared.

The five of them stood there awkwardly for a moment, each of them embarrassed and scared. Albert noticed from the corner of his eye that only Beverly was not trying to hide her nudity. While the others stood with their hands covering their privates and their bodies turned away from one another, she stood straight and proud, with her hands clenched at her sides. Perhaps she was too distracted by whatever it was she felt in this place to be concerned with modesty, or perhaps she just refused to be embarrassed of her nudity when she was so much older than the rest of them.

Nicole stood with her back against the cold, stone wall, one hand timidly covering her naked crotch, the other arm crossed over her breasts. "So do we swim now?" She asked.

Albert glanced at her, but it was only a glance. This

was incredibly uncomfortable. After his last experience in these corridors, he would have thought that he'd be used to something like this, but being here naked with only Brandy had been much different. Even though he had hardly known her, there was something more natural about standing unclothed in front of a single member of the opposite sex. Being in a group like this was strange. And surprisingly enough, he felt that being naked in front of Wayne and Beverly, who were virtually strangers, was not as bad as being naked in front of Nicole, and seeing her like that, even from the corner of his eye while she kept herself covered, made him feel almost sick with a combination of childish curiosity and guilt. His sex drive, still in overdrive from the first night he came here, made him want to look at her, to see her, to relish the beauty of her nakedness, but his relationship to her, and more importantly to Brandy, made the idea of even snatching a glance in her direction seem like absolute betrayal. Though she was a beautiful woman, she was still his friend, a good friend, almost family. He forced his eyes forward instead, into the darkness that hung over the cold, still water, and then nodded. "We swim now," he confirmed.

He looked at Brandy, who stood with her arms crossed over her breasts and her body turned toward him and away from the others. She was hiding from Wayne, he knew. The only member of the opposite sex present besides her own lover. He glanced at him, saw that he was standing back from everyone, his hands crossed over his groin, his eyes fixed awkwardly on a random place low on the wall, as though the stone there was suddenly very interesting to him, and he felt a surprisingly intense surge of jealousy. He fixed his eyes on Brandy and tried to focus his attention on the task at hand. “Ready?”

Brandy nodded. She was as ready as she was ever going to be.

Chapter 8

In thirteen months the water had gotten no warmer. Albert and Brandy braved the cold together, hand in hand, as they did the first time, their naked bodies shivering before their knees were even wet.

"Oh god!" Brandy hissed. She was squeezing his hand hard enough to leave marks with her fingernails, but he barely felt it over the icy torture of the water.

Albert glanced back at the others. Nicole was right behind them, still covering herself, her teeth clenched against the biting cold that was climbing up her calves. Behind her, Beverly had also stepped into the water. Her arms were crossed over her bosom, but less for modesty than for warmth. Wayne was still on dry stone, watching them, probably contemplating turning back after all. That would have been all right. Albert hardly would have blamed him. And that adolescent jealousy lurking within him made him wish that he would.

The water climbed with icy fingers up their naked legs and thighs. The cold could have been a solid thing, gripping and biting.

A long, pitiful whine rose from Nicole's throat as the water touched the lower curves of her buttocks and Albert reached back to her with the hand that held his flashlight. She relinquished some of her modesty and took the hand, gripping his wrist so that he could still hold the light.

"So your name is Wayne," Beverly said through clenched teeth as the water numbed her thighs and sent gooseflesh rippling across her body.

Wayne had finally begun to move and the water was like mild torture against his skin. "Yeah," he replied, hardly in the mood to chat with her.

"I really am sorry about the others. I never thought four people wouldn't come out of there."

"Well they didn't." Wayne held not an ounce of

compassion for this woman.

Beverly opened her mouth to say more, but closed it. She could feel tears welling up in her eyes. Wayne was not going to forgive her, not now, not anytime soon. He was never going to trust her. His dislike for her radiated from him. She would count herself lucky if he didn't kill her while they were down here…and that was probably just what she really deserved.

Ahead, Albert, Brandy and Nicole were submerged to their chests. A few steps more and they began to swim.

The five of them struggled through the water, trying to hold onto their flashlights as they battled the cold. Brandy had left her backpack with her clothes. The jackets would have been useless once they'd gotten wet anyway, and they apparently wouldn't need the swimwear. She carried nothing on her but her flashlight, her glasses and her jewelry.

Moments later—though it seemed much longer—they stepped out of the pool, their shivering bodies dripping. Albert kissed Brandy on the lips. "You did great," he told her. His voice stuttered with the violence of his shivers. He glanced back at Nicole. "You too."

Nicole still held his wrist, squeezing it as though she meant to sap the heat from his body. With her other hand, she wiped her wet hair from her face and the water from her eyes, leaving her entire body exposed long enough for Albert to see her.

His eyes held on her breasts for a brief moment before he forced them away, embarrassed and ashamed. He was not interested in Nicole's body, certainly not when he was so in love with Brandy. His eyes had wandered innocently, as though he were admiring her pretty new dress or a lovely necklace. Besides, after his swim he was hardly aroused. Still, he felt guilty.

"It was nice of that guy to skim the ice off the water before we got in," Wayne said as he splashed onto the dry stone.

"I hope none of us catch pneumonia down here," Nicole said, wiping more water from her brow. Over the summer Albert had seen her in a bikini on several occasions and he knew she had a knockout body, but seeing her completely naked was different. Her breasts were not merely large, but firm and round. She still had faint tan lines from summer and a mole on her belly just above and to the right of her navel.

Without their clothes, Albert realized that Brandy and Nicole's jewelry was much more accentuated against their skin. Nicole was wearing a gold necklace with a small, heart-shaped charm that dangled near the sexy cleft between the upper curves of her breasts. On her left wrist, she wore a silver watch and on her right was a single silver and gold bracelet that twinkled prettily in the glow of the flashlights. In addition, she wore two rings on each hand and three pairs of earrings, two in her lobes and one near the upper arch of her ears. Looking at these earrings now, Albert wondered if he'd ever really noticed them before. He certainly had never thought about them consciously. Perhaps it was merely his desire to find something besides her naked body to focus his thoughts on. He turned his eyes back to Brandy, who was still wearing the same three rings and watch that she'd had when he first met her, her favorite items, but was now also wearing his high school ring on her left thumb. Also, the necklace he had given her for her birthday just two weeks before was now dangling from her pretty neck. It was a small golden rose on a fine chain, not expensive by any real means but very pretty. She was also still wearing one of the bracelets he had bought her last Christmas and only a single pair of earrings.

"We'll be fine," Albert assured her, turning his eyes away from her and looking quickly back at their other two companions. He was not used to trying to keep his eyes in one place. He liked to observe everything around him, take in his surroundings. Now he felt ashamed just trying to see if everyone was out of the water. "We'll warm up when we get moving."

Beverly was not nearly as beautiful as the young women whose company she now shared, but she was not entirely unattractive. Though her face seemed hard and bitter with age, her body was still firm. She was very skinny, with small and rather unimpressive breasts, and with the exception of some faint color on her arms and face, her skin was so pale that Albert found the copious black hair between her legs startlingly visible. She remained completely uninterested in hiding her nudity.

Unlike Brandy and Nicole, she wore very little jewelry. Only a watch with a brown leather strap and a single sapphire ring on her right ring finger adorned her bare body. Her ears didn't even appear to be pierced.

Then there was Wayne, his body broad, strong but not really toned. He was a little thick around the gut, but not exactly fat. He was a formidable man who, Albert was sure, would impress and intimidate much more adequately when warmer. He was rubbing his arms for warmth and looking anywhere to keep from looking at the naked women around him. He wore no jewelry at all, not even a watch.

Albert turned his eyes to Brandy, his girlfriend, his lover, and another pang of jealousy ran through him at the idea that Wayne could see her naked. It was a childish feeling. After all, he had now seen Nicole naked. Perhaps it was only fair that there be another man down here too. Besides, why should he have to feel jealous? Brandy loved him. She would never leave him. He would always be the one to lie beside her at night. And so what if Wayne had now seen her naked? He was not the first, after all. Brandy had had lovers before him, and they didn't keep him awake at night. They had no reason to. But, considering this, he wondered how Brandy felt about him being able to see Nicole and even Beverly nude.

“Then maybe we should get moving,” Brandy suggested through violently chattering teeth, and Albert saw the way her eyes intentionally avoided everybody. She looked as though she’d suddenly become fascinated with everyone’s feet.

Albert nodded. “Yeah.” He focused his thoughts back onto the temple and the journey ahead. This would take some getting used to, but there was no reason to let it keep them from what they came to do. “We’ve got a long way to go.”

The five of them moved on, still shivering, still dripping, up the gentle slope of the tunnel.

“I still say this isn’t right,” said Wayne. “Even if there was something in that water that completely erased any scent from our bodies, which I highly doubt, then we’ll still start to smell again real soon. No matter how cold we are now, we’re bound to start sweating sometime.”

“I understand taking our underwear,” Albert said. “He puts it in the maze where we’ll cross later and attracts the hounds to that area, away from our path. But you’re right. I don’t know why we couldn’t keep the rest of our clothes." Albert found that focusing on *why* they had to be naked, along with the biting cold, helped to keep his mind off *being* naked, so he embraced it.

"Maybe it's just a rule," suggested Nicole. "Like how they used to make the athletes compete naked in the early Olympics."

"It's possible," agreed Albert. "And you have to admit, we're more comfortable naked and soaking wet than in our jeans and soaking wet."

"That's true," agreed Wayne. He hated the feel of wet blue jeans.

"Doesn't really matter now, does it," Brandy said.

"I guess it doesn't," agreed Albert.

As she tried to warm up, Nicole found herself thinking about their nudity and the fact that she and Albert had now seen each other naked. It was an odd thing to think. He was the only man to see her naked since she was a child who had not had sex with her. She wondered how it would be now, knowing every time she saw him that he'd seen her naked, knowing what *he* looked like naked, yet never having been in any kind of relationship with him that defined such knowledge of each other. Would it be awkward? Would she always wonder if he was remembering the way she looked, relishing the image in his mind? Would she learn to resent him? She did not think that she could ever resent Albert, but people had a way of changing and she was no exception. She had done a lot of changing already in her young life.

Wayne was surprised at himself. Had he been told that two beautiful young women were going to strip down to their birthday suits right in front of him, he first of all would not have believed a word of it, and secondly would have thought that it was going to be one hell of a show. But now that they were all here, he found himself looking anywhere but at them. He felt like a child who has been told that the lady on the movie screen is undressing so he'd better close his eyes.

Up ahead, a drop-off appeared. Albert and Brandy gazed apprehensively into the lower tunnel. It was from here that they had been chased thirteen months ago by what must have been one of the hounds the blind man warned them about. The round room with the statue of the dying sentinels waited a short distance ahead. Beyond that was the hate room.

Albert dropped down into this lower tunnel and shined his light into the darkness ahead. There was nothing but the few scattered bone fragments he'd observed long ago. The floor was still marred by the scratches he remembered agonizing over. *The hounds*, he thought. Did they have something to do with those scratches? *The hounds are fast, but they cannot jump.* That explained the wall behind him. If they could not jump then they could not get from the lower stretch of this tunnel to the higher. It would also explain why it stopped chasing them last time.

Once he was convinced that the path was clear, he placed his flashlight on the ledge beside him and then held his hands up to his waiting girlfriend. "Come on down."

Brandy sat down with her feet dangling over the ledge in front of him, and took both his hands. With a swift and graceful motion, she hopped down in front of him.

Albert then turned and held his hands out to Nicole.

She hesitated for a moment, standing at the edge of

the upper tunnel, looking down at him, her hands crossed over her private areas. She did not want him to help her down because to do so, she would have to give him her hands and that would allow him to see her. He had certainly seen what she had by now anyway, but her modesty was stubborn. She braced herself and sat down in front of him, just as Brandy had done. She reminded herself that they were at least on an even playing field. She only had to lower her eyes a few degrees to get a good look at him. And what did it really matter in the greater scheme of things if she let him see her naked? It wouldn't really change anything, would it? Biting her lip, feeling just like the virgin who once stripped her clothes off for her high school boyfriend, Josh, she held both hands out to him.

He took her hands and she hopped down into the lower tunnel with him. When she was on her feet, she smiled sweetly at him and then walked past him to make room for the others. He had looked her right in the eye, with the same respect, tenderness and love with which he always looked at her, and she found that she loved Albert Cross like she might have loved her own brother if she had one, perhaps even more.

Albert turned and held his hands out to Beverly, who had approached the edge and was looking down at him. When she saw him reaching, she backed away, her eyes wide and terrified. The very thought of him touching her seemed to fill her with inexplicable panic. And yet he had not once even spoken harshly to her. He pulled his hands back, holding them up as if to say, "Okay, have it your way," and backed away.

Beverly sat down and dropped into the tunnel, turning a little on her right side as she did so to keep from hurting her left wrist any more than she already had. Wayne dropped down behind her, not bothering to sit down as the others had, but merely leveraging himself on one hand. It was very manly, but he winced when he landed. Perhaps he'd forgotten that he was no longer wearing his tennis shoes.

Albert retrieved his flashlight from the ledge. "This is where the hounds are," he warned. "We should hurry."

The five of them moved quickly through the tunnel, their bare feet slapping the hard stone as they walked. Up ahead, the round room—the *decision* room, as Albert thought it—came into view.

Albert hardly looked at the statue in the center of the room. The blue cloth was still there, wrapped around one of the sentinels' hands, right where he'd left it, but he didn't need it. He turned left and headed straight for the first tunnel clockwise of the one from which they exited. "Come on," he urged the others. He remembered the way he and Brandy had lingered at this crossroad, pondering the statue and its meaning, the destination of the other tunnels and the scratches on the floor. He remembered hearing the thing in the next tunnel and wondered how close they'd come to being just more scattered bone fragments in these passages. Their scent was probably what lured it. The risk of their lack of speed was sickening now that he was aware of it.

They hurried up the next passage to the wall that supposedly kept the hounds bound to these passages. Albert stopped and helped Brandy up, then Nicole. Like before, he held a hand out to Beverly, not really thinking anything, but merely trying to be courteous, and like before, she recoiled from his hand as if it were a venomous snake. He stepped back—still not understanding her terror of him, but yielding just the same—and simply watched her help herself.

Once all of them were in the next tunnel, Albert gazed down into the lower one from which they'd just climbed. He remembered wondering why those scratches were down there, but not up here. Unless there was something else down here that was restricted to only these corridors, they almost certainly were somehow related to the hounds.

The hounds.

Albert felt his flesh crawl at the thought of the very word.

"The hate room's just up there," Brandy said to Albert. "Do you think we can get through it again?"

"I don't see why *we* can't," he replied, meaning the two of them. "We got through it last time. We didn't feel a thing." He also thought Nicole would have no trouble passing through the hate room, but he was not certain about Beverly or Wayne. He was still not sure how these rooms worked, if they simply put visions into your head and subliminally told you to do things, or if they somehow heightened what was already inside. Perhaps he and Brandy had felt nothing because neither of them was capable of feeling hate toward each other. If that were the case, then he worried about Wayne. His rage had not gone unnoticed, after all. Beverly, on the other hand, was a wild card. He was not sure what would happen when she went in there, regardless of how it all worked.

As they stepped into the entrance of the hate room, its size and shape identical to that of the entrance to the sex room, the five of them marveled again at the impressiveness of its very existence.

Beverly stopped walking as she took in the vastness of the chamber and Wayne, with his eyes fixed on the statues to his left, bumped into her. She stepped away from him, flinching, and for the first time he seemed to not have any violence in him.

"I'm sorry," he said softly. "My fault." Perhaps it had been her eyes that kept him from telling her to watch what the fuck she was doing, that look of a frightened child who's just spilled a glass of Kool-Aid on the carpet and knows she's in for a scolding, perhaps even a beating. Suddenly he felt very ashamed of himself.

Beverly did not speak to him. She merely shrank

away from him, although careful not to go in Albert's direction.

"Who gets the glasses this time?" Nicole asked as she walked toward the far wall, curious to see the face that would lead them into hate.

"I might be able to do this one," Albert volunteered.

Ahead, the enraged face of a man materialized out of the darkness and Nicole paused, as if startled by it. Albert did not doubt that she was. The face had not lost a bit of its ferocity in the last thirteen months.

Chapter 9

"This room isn't much bigger than the last one," Albert told the others as he peered into the shadows beyond the angry man's open mouth. "I think if we keep our eyes closed we should do okay. But the room on the other side is a spiked pit. If one of us goes through that other doorway without looking…well, you don't need me to tell you." He held his hand out to Brandy, who removed her glasses and handed them to him. "We'll take it slow and easy. I'll tell you all when to stop. There's five of us, so we can't just pile out of there, okay?" He took Brandy's hand as he donned her glasses. "How do I look?"

Brandy leaned close to him so that she could see and

then giggled at the sight.

Nicole, without thinking about it, dropped her eyes from Albert's face to his privates and then blushed furiously. She did not know what possessed her to do such a thing. She would never have thought herself capable of sneaking a peek at her best friend's boyfriend like that, but there it was. Literally. She was immediately filled with guilt, yet she realized that, even as she was thinking this, she was still looking at that part of him! She tore her eyes away and looked at Brandy instead, terrified that she'd seen her in spite of her nearsightedness, but Brandy was still looking at Albert and grinning at how silly he looked wearing her glasses and nothing more.

Wayne was looking back at the last pair of statues in the room. These sentinels were running at each other in a blind rage, frozen mid-stride as they raced murderously toward each other. Even without faces, their fury was unmistakable. They were going to kill each other. "So what's the plan in case you're wrong about Beverly? What do we do if she turns psycho on us?"

Albert removed Brandy's glasses and looked at Beverly. She stood apart from the rest of them, her hands balled into fists at her sides. He could tell by the look on her face that she was scared. He supposed there was only one answer to that, but he did not want to say it aloud.

"The rest of us will be blind," Brandy reminded him. "If she loses control…"

"Wayne can stop me," Beverly said.

Nicole looked at Wayne. "Can you?"

"I don't know," Wayne confessed. He glanced back at the statues. "If she's completely consumed by rage… I'm not confident I can hold her."

"I didn't say you can hold me," Beverly corrected him. "I said you can *stop* me."

Wayne stared at her, hardly believing what she was suggesting.

"Any way you have to." She was staring intently at him. "You can hurt me. You already did it once."

"That was—"

"Justified," she finished for him. "Just remember what happened to those kids in Gilbert House. I deserve it."

Wayne stared at her. He did not know what to say. He did not really want to hurt her. He was not proud of himself for how he'd treated her, regardless of whether she deserved it or not. But he also did not want anyone else to get hurt.

"You can stop me," she said again. "I don't want to hurt anyone else." She held her hand out to him and he wrapped his strong fingers firmly around her wrist.

"We'll see," was all Wayne could think to say.

Albert nodded. "Okay then. You two will take the rear again. If anything happens, we'll all be counting on Wayne."

Wayne didn't look very confident, but it seemed like the only option they had.

Albert slipped Brandy's glasses back onto his face and gave her hand a reassuring squeeze as he turned to face the hate room. "Ready?"

Everyone was. Brandy had no belt loop for Nicole to grasp the way Brandy had done in the sex room, so she put her free hand instead on her friend's waist and followed. As she ducked into the angry man's mouth, she felt Wayne's hand fall upon her shoulder, and when she glanced back, she saw that he was still gripping Beverly's good wrist. If she began to lose control, she would have to wrench herself free of his hand, which would give him the opportunity to turn on her.

Wayne felt incredibly uncomfortable. He did not know what he'd do if Beverly went crazy. He supposed the simplest thing would be to tackle her to the floor and hold her there while the others made their way safely past the spike pit in the next room. But then what would he do? He was just going to have to play it by ear.

Connected by a touch, the five of them made their way slowly into the hate room.

Through his girlfriend's glasses, Albert saw shades of gray fading in and out of the darkness. Shapes reached out to him from the gloom, many visible enough to be recognized for what they were. He saw hands and faces and sometimes whole human forms of various sizes and frozen in many different poses, but none possessed any real detail through these lenses, and were therefore unable to infect him with their rage. This was what Brandy had seen all those months ago, while his eyes were firmly closed. He marveled at this, thankful that he had the opportunity to walk in her shoes (or in her eyes, as the case may be).

He made his way around a statue that was certainly human, but could have been of either sex and doing almost anything. Brandy's glasses worked, but Nicole was right. They were a little too small for this. He had to consciously force his eyes to remain straight ahead. It was far too easy to peek around the sides or over the top. "How's everybody doing so far?" he asked.

"I'm fine," Brandy replied.

"Me too," Nicole reported.

"I think I'm okay," Beverly said, sounding reassuringly confident. "I don't see anything yet."

"Good," Albert replied. "Wayne?"

"I'm okay," Wayne assured him, and Albert felt a wave of relief. If it was going to do anything to them, it at least hadn't started yet.

Albert pushed forward. As he moved deeper into the chamber, he became more and more aware of the space around Brandy's glasses. No matter how hard he tried, his eyes kept twitching toward the edges of the lenses. From the corners of his eyes he could see the statues around him, and had to force himself to stare straight ahead, knowing that terrible things could happen if he let his eyes stray left or right. For all he knew, just one peek could fill him with hatred every bit as insatiable as the lust that overwhelmed him on his first visit. He squinted his eyes almost closed, trying to rid himself of as much of his peripheral vision as he could, and lifted his chin to keep from peering over the glasses.

"Beverly," Wayne began, "why did you pick me to give that letter to?"

"I told you, you just looked the part. I needed someone with some muscle."

"But there's lots of people in this town bigger than me."

"But lots of people didn't leave their stuff unguarded in the library where I could drop that letter off without them seeing me."

"I see." And he did. He had expected as much, after all. "I was just in the wrong place at the wrong time."

"I'm sorry," she said and he actually believed that she was sincere. "I gave you and two other guys those letters. I thought that if three big guys like you showed up and went in there, you would probably come back out. Only one of you came, though, and he showed up with three friends. I…know I shouldn't have let them go in… but I had to know…and I thought they might be okay. Only one of them was big like you, but I thought…maybe since there're *four* of them…"

"But why," asked Albert, "would you even bother with three random people if you had that picture of Wendell Gilbert? Why didn't you just send me the envelope? Why not just come find me? If you'd been honest with me I'd have gone in." The truth of this actually sent a shiver through Albert. Had she come to him instead of bothering with Wayne and the others, things probably would have turned out much differently. And not likely in a good way.

For a moment, Beverly did not speak, and when she did finally reply, it was not an answer: "I…couldn't do that."

Albert did not know what she meant by that, but he did not push the matter.

The five of them walked on, moving slowly through the darkness. Albert focused on keeping his eyes forced straight ahead, trying not to look around the glasses, no matter how paranoid he grew or how curious he became.

But it was not easy. Whenever a shape emerged from the darkness, his first instinct was to peek, to see what it was, whether it was important, if it had any meaning. After all, wasn't it his skill with puzzles that led him here in the first place? He loved to solve mysteries. He prided himself on his skills of observation. It went against his nature to intentionally ignore details.

A shape took form on his left and his eyes twitched toward it. He glimpsed a woman's face with a cruel grin and laughing eyes. There was something odd about this face, but he refused to focus on it. He forced his eyes forward again and tried to ignore it, but even after it was behind him and out of sight, the face lingered in his thoughts. He didn't like that face. It was the expression, he thought, something about that mocking sneer.

Something hot began to grow in his stomach. It was subtle, but he could feel it. It wasn't all that different from what he'd felt in the sex room, but this wasn't lust. This was anger.

He forced the woman's face from his thoughts. It was so easy to fall into that trap, but he refused. Instead, he thought about the other room, the sex room, what he and Brandy did in there the last time they were here. He remembered how she looked just before she lost control, her blue eyes wide as she stared upon that furious orgy of stone men and women, her knees bent, her hand pressed against the front of her jeans, unable to control the furious desire that was sweeping through her like a wildfire.

The hot anger in his gut was lost beneath a hotter feeling now, and he welcomed it. He reminded himself that Brandy was naked again, just like last time, her lovely body fully exposed. Then he reminded himself that Nicole was naked, too, that her incredible breasts were right there, completely uncovered. He could look at her if he wanted. Her eyes were closed. She'd never see him as he studied her in the beam of his flashlight, memorizing her luscious curves.

He'd never do such a thing, of course, and not just because he'd risk seeing more of the hate room's statues. He wouldn't do it because he had more respect for Nicole than that, because he was her friend and he cared about her, because he loved Brandy far too much, but it didn't hurt to think about such things. In fact, it helped. That sick feeling in his belly was completely gone now, replaced by something considerably more pleasant (although with the rather embarrassing side-effect of giving him a noticeable erection).

He tried to clear his mind as he focused on the path ahead. Another statue stood ahead of him and he squeezed his eyes into narrow slits to avoid seeing anything more than gray blobs in the gloom as he passed.

He asked if everyone was still doing okay.

Everyone replied that they were fine.

"I guess you were right," Beverly said. "I can't see any statues. All I see in my head are…shades of gray."

"Which is exactly what I see," Albert marveled. It seemed to him that, being psychic, she probably had some sort of mysterious ability to see what others saw. Brandy saw all of the statues when she first entered the sex room and, because she was with them in her dreams that night, so did Beverly. When Brandy tried to pass through the sex room the second time, she remembered the things she saw the first time. The blurry shapes somehow retained their meaning, even though her sight was significantly hindered. This time, when Nicole used

Brandy's glasses, she was able to pass through it with ease because she could not discern the shapes she saw through them. But Beverly could both see what Nicole was seeing and remember the statues from her dream. She had no memories of these statues because none of them had ever seen them.

Of course, this was nothing more than a theory. He had no way of knowing how Beverly's psychic abilities worked or how these rooms worked. The important thing was that Beverly was not feeling anything from the hate room.

But Wayne did not loosen his grip on Beverly's wrist. He was relieved that she was still in control of herself, but he did not dare take the chance that she might still lose it.

Albert was just beginning to wonder if he'd somehow become turned around when he finally caught sight of the opening that led out of the hate room. Relieved, he turned his attention on the danger that lurked just beyond that doorway. "I think this is it," he said, moving toward the exit. "Remember, don't anybody push or I'm a pincushion."

Brandy squeezed his hand tightly, not at all liking the mental image of him tumbling into those hateful spikes.

"Okay. We're here. Just stop and wait a minute. Don't open your eyes."

Albert stepped through the doorway and removed Brandy's glasses. Ahead of him, just as he remembered, the floor dropped off into a deadly pit of wicked stone spikes. The mere sight of them was enough to drive all other thoughts from his mind.

He stepped cautiously onto the narrow ledge and sidled away from the door. He then turned and gave Brandy her glasses back. "We'll go one at a time."

Brandy put her glasses on and looked down. She could almost feel the tips of those awful spikes. Without getting any closer to the pit than necessary, she followed Albert out of the hate room. Behind her, Nicole did the same.

"That's not even funny," Wayne observed, staring at the spiked pit.

"Nothing about this place is funny," Brandy said.

Albert ducked into the next passage, still holding onto Brandy's hand. Behind them, Nicole followed close.

With the dangers finally behind them, Wayne relinquished his grip on Beverly's arm and entered the next passage behind the others. But Beverly did not immediately follow. Instead, she lingered there, her eyes fixed on the spikes. They were terrible things, wickedly sharp. One of those had the potential to pass right through a human being and find no resistance at all. It was difficult to look into this pit and not picture a human body lying at the bottom.

But these grisly imaginings were not what made her pause to reflect upon the pit. As she stared at it, she felt a strange sensation, as though there was something important about it, something very significant, as though she had seen it somewhere before, and not when Albert and Brandy were here. It was like something from an old nightmare that she couldn't quite remember.

Albert, Brandy and Nicole stood in the next chamber, their flashlights scanning the walls. "I remember this room," said Albert. "It doesn't make any sense. It's like they forgot to furnish it or something."

Nicole studied the blank walls and ceiling. Albert had talked of this room a few times, the room that he'd found curiously pointless, and it was not hard to see why. It was just an empty square room, a little more than fifteen feet across, with a tall ceiling and another narrow passage on the opposite side that was identical to the one from which they'd just entered. It served no apparent purpose.

"I don't know what it's for," Albert said, still bothered by it, but not willing to spend much time on it. Perhaps it was nothing. Maybe it was simply here to allow travelers to rest once they'd conquered the hate room. Or maybe this was where the survivors of that room could conveniently finish killing each other should they make it all the way past the spiked pit in their blind rage. There was no way he was likely to understand the minds of those who built this place. He began to walk toward the next passage and Brandy and Nicole followed.

Wayne crossed the room behind them, shining his flashlight onto the walls and ceiling, relieved to be safely past the perils of the hate room and its deadly pit.

Beverly at last pulled her eyes away from the gruesome spikes and ducked into the short passage to catch up with the others. She was still thinking about that pit, about how easily fragile life could be torn from its shell by such a thing, and wondering why she found it so vividly significant and appalling. A horrible shiver had begun to creep up her spine. She glanced back at it once more, and could almost see blood dripping down the wicked skewers. She suddenly wanted to get as far from that room as she could. That place had the morbid feel of an open grave. It was a bad place. She turned away from it, not wanting anything more to do with it, and peered into the "empty" room through which her young companions were already passing.

Her shriek was heart-stopping. Startled, Wayne spun to face her, certain that some murderous horror had appeared from an unseen crevice. Albert, Nicole and Brandy likewise turned to see, their eyes wide and afraid.

Beverly was standing just within the passage, screaming at the top of her lungs at something above them, her terrified eyes almost bulging with fright. She staggered backward, as though something were attacking her, but there was nothing there. The room was still empty.

She whipped her head back, as if an invisible snake

had just struck at her face. The top of her head struck the passage's ceiling, but she didn't seem to notice. She crossed her arms over her eyes, protecting herself from whatever it was that was terrifying her, or perhaps just blocking out whatever horrible vision had instilled such terror.

Wayne stared at her, unable to understand what had frightened her. The room was silent except for her shrieking. There was nothing at all. The room was empty. But Beverly did not seem to believe that. She staggered backward, through the passage from which she'd come, and Wayne suddenly realized that she was going to back right into the pit.

He bolted toward her, his voice joining hers as he cried out for her to stop.

Albert, too, bolted after her as he realized what was about to happen, leaving the girls to stand and gawk in horror at the spectacle before them.

Beverly did not see any of them. Her arms were crossed over her eyes, her face hidden, still screaming, still lost in a storm of unthinkable terror as she backed toward the very pit from which she had not been able to pull her eyes only seconds before. She did not hear Wayne's shouts of warning, did not realize that one more step would tumble her into those giant stone needles and silence her screams forever.

Wayne rushed through the short passage, his arms outstretched, reaching out for her as her heel rocked off the edge of the pit. He saw her begin to sway back, her arms parting slightly as the realization of what was about to happen seemed to come to her. He snatched at her, his fingers grazing her arm and her breast, feeling for one second the cool touch of her bare skin…but nothing more.

She had thought, just moments ago, that the deadly room had the eerie, significant feel of a grave. *Her* grave. Her tomb. She had been psychic her entire life, at the mercy of keen, otherworldly senses she never wanted. It had always tortured her, and in the end, when it could have saved her, it utterly failed her. She did not recognize her own death in that wicked pit, only the horror of death in general. The deep warning of the queer, personal significance of this very spot had, in fact, fatally distracted her.

Beverly Bridger, and all of her mysteries, fell…and her screams were silenced in one sickening instant.

Albert caught up with Wayne, but could only stand beside him and stare. Beverly lay in the pit, her head tilted up a little, one hand propped up by the wrist on one spike, the other, her hurt one, lying on the floor beside her. Six separate spikes protruded from her belly and chest, another from her neck. One came right through her left breast, misshaping it slightly as her body's weight pulled her down onto it. Three had gone through her left thigh and another through the calf. Her right leg was sticking up in the air, one of the spikes having torn a gash from the back of her knee to her ankle as she fell. Blood flowed slowly from her punctured body and spread around her in a gruesome pool. Her flashlight lay at the bottom of the pit, a few feet from her body, illuminating the whole gory scene.

The two of them stared for a moment, unable to speak or act.

"I tried to save her," Wayne said, almost absently. He felt numb with shock. He felt as though he'd suddenly fallen asleep and begun to dream.

“I know,” Albert assured him. “That was good of you.” He put his hand on Wayne’s shoulder. “It’s okay.”

“What happened?” Brandy asked. She and Nicole were standing at the other end of the tunnel, unwilling to come any closer. Her tone told him that she already knew.

“She’s dead,” Albert said, his voice sounding very far away to himself.

“Oh my god…” Nicole sounded sick. “What happened?” She knew, of course, what killed her. Her imagination was brutally honest on that subject. She didn’t need to look into that pit to know that she had fallen victim to those ghastly spikes. But what brought her to that end? It was as though she had suddenly gone crazy again, the way she did when Albert had reached out to help her in the entrance to the sex room, his only intention to try and help her.

Albert shook his head. He honestly had no idea. He turned and walked away from the bloody scene, back to Brandy and Nicole, who each looked as shocked as he felt.

For a long time, Wayne stood staring at Beverly’s

naked and lifeless body. He remembered grabbing her outside of Gilbert House, remembered slinging her around and hurling her into the brush, tearing the buttons from her shirt and spraining her wrist. Later, he had been no gentler when he threw her to the floor in the entrance to the sex room. He had even jerked her out of the sex room after she nearly lost control, his temper flaring, hating her for even being alive.

And now she was dead.

Brandy and Nicole stood together, silent and shocked, unable to believe what had transpired. It happened so quickly. She was literally just here. And now she was gone forever. Albert put his arms around them both, unable to get the image of her lifeless body out of his head.

What the hell happened? Why did she begin screaming like that? It didn't make sense. There was nothing in this room, not even one of those faceless sentinel statues. He looked up at the dark ceiling, the place where her terrified eyes had fixed before she covered her face and retreated to her death.

"I'm sorry," Wayne said softly, speaking to Beverly.

He *was* sorry. He was damn sorry. He didn't feel like he'd ever loved himself, but now he was beginning to feel like the most insufferable ass who ever lived. He had tragically failed two women in only a few short hours.

In the silence, Albert stared up at the ceiling, looking at the darkness, looking *into* it. Perhaps there was more here than met the eye, perhaps this room was not so pointless or empty after all.

Wayne turned away, leaving Beverly behind him, and joined the others. For a moment, he stood next to them as they held each other in an intimate silence. Then, without saying a word, he walked past them, toward the next tunnel. Nicole followed after him, her heart breaking at the sight of his misery, and Brandy followed next.

Albert hesitated, still staring at the ceiling. Beverly had told them that she was psychic. Did that give her a wider perspective of the world? Were there things out there that she could see that were hidden from the eyes of others?

He walked across the room to the passage his friends had already entered. He ducked inside, then paused and looked back. Perhaps it was his imagination, but for just an instant, he thought he heard something, a soft sound, sort of like chains rattling in the distance.

Chapter 10

"What's that noise?" Wayne felt as though he were struggling with sleep, his thoughts refusing to focus, his every movement sluggish. He had done no more than walk across the room and duck into the next tunnel, had walked only perhaps twenty or twenty-five yards from where Beverly's body lay, yet the world had slowed almost to a stop and not minutes but hours seemed to have passed. This thick emptiness into which he was sinking was comforting, like death to the sick and weary, yet there was something wrong with the emptiness. There was that noise, like a frenzied buzzing of bees somewhere nearby and growing closer.

"The hounds," Albert replied, his voice as distant as

the ocean to Wayne's ears.

The hounds, Wayne thought. *The hounds are deaf and blind but they smell. The hounds are fast, but they can't jump. The hounds are…* What? What were the hounds? To him they were just the words of some creepy old blind man, but what *were* they? What was that god-awful sound they were making? They were some sort of dog, he suspected, perhaps bald and eyeless like the man who made them leave their clothes behind. *What are they doing?* He wondered, lost in his own head.

"Wayne?" Nicole's voice, soft and soothing. "Are you okay?"

Nicole was pretty. *Very* pretty. She was nice, too. He liked her. He mentally shook himself, clearing his head a little. "Yeah," he replied. He looked at her, actually focusing his eyes on something for the first time since turning away from Beverly's body. She was walking beside him, her brilliant eyes fixed on his, genuine concern painted on her pretty face. She was still naked, still lovely, still alive.

He snapped back a little, as though splashed with cool water. She *was* still alive. So were Albert and

Brandy. So was *he*, damn it! If he was going to stay that way, and he intended to for a while yet, then he was going to have to just bottle what happened to Beverly.

"You sure?" Nicole had stopped trying to hide her nudity. Her breasts swayed voluptuously as she walked and he realized as he noticed this that he'd forgotten completely about being naked, his own body just as revealed as hers.

"Yeah. I'm okay." He suddenly felt very self-conscious and insecure. As he felt his neck grow hot with a blush, he realized that he really wasn't okay. He was in shock, his mind running on auxiliary power alone. For reasons he could not understand, he thought of Laura Swiff and her muddy green eyes and short, black hair.

"He'll come back to us," Albert assured Nicole.

The four of them—four once again—stepped out of the tunnel. The enormous stone bridge stretched out in front of them. Four sentinels and three more tunnels waited at its far end. Beneath them, the shadowy maze stood like the ruins of an ancient city, stretching out seemingly forever into the darkness. The hounds rattled and shuffled and clicked unseen in the shadows between those walls. To Albert and Brandy, it was as awesome a sight as the first night they looked upon it, and to Nicole, it surpassed her wildest dreams.

To the right and far below, the noise of the hounds was concentrated. A chaos of noise rose from the base of an enormous stone column. Buzzing, clicking, grinding. Above this racket of what was certainly a great many creatures, aligned in a neat row, were five pairs of socks. Five pairs of underpants were hung above them and three bras were hung above these. The blind man had arranged them together, just as he'd done the last time. Brandy's pink bra was just above her little, pink thong and Nicole's lacy black bra and matching panties were equally displayed, as was Beverly's mismatch of white bra and flowered panties. To creatures whose only eyes and ears were their noses, it must have seemed that five people were hanging there, tantalizingly out of their reach, taunting them.

"I can't see them," Nicole said, gazing down into the shadows.

"Maybe that's a good thing," Albert said. He stared for a moment longer at their undergarments, at that price they'd all paid to safely pass these mysterious creatures, and then continued on across the bridge.

The four sentinels still stood their ground, still stared blankly ahead and still refused to offer help to any weary travelers, but Albert already knew which of the three tunnels would lead them forward and not down into that terrible place below or to some other unthinkable fate.

Wayne and Brandy started forward after Albert, but Nicole lagged behind, fascinated by the maze and all its mysteries. "Wasn't there a Greek hero who faced the Minotaur in a place like this?"

Albert paused, his eyes drawn to the walls far below. "Yeah," he said. He felt as though the air around him had just grown a little thinner. It was an easy thing to picture, a fantastic thing to wonder. Of course this wasn't the same place. That was preposterous. But the idea had a magical quality to it. "I don't remember the story, really, but—"

"The Labyrinth of Crete," Wayne said, as if in a daze. He, too, had stopped and was staring down at the dark walls below. "An enormous, spiraling maze, with no way out. It was underground, and in the center was the monster, half man, half bull. It lived on the flesh of sacrificial victims."

Everyone had turned and was staring at him as though he'd just performed some fantastic magic trick.

"The hero who slew him was Theseus." He looked up at Albert with eyes that were still a little dim. "You look surprised."

Albert shrugged. "Didn't know you were into mythology."

"I do a lot of reading."

Albert looked down at the maze beneath them. "It's not really spiraling, though, is it?"

"And porcupines don't really throw their quills," Wayne replied.

Albert stared down into the shadowy maze. Wayne was right. Facts got lost and exaggerated, especially over time. It was easy to imagine that this was the mythical Labyrinth of Crete, far away from where historians would have it placed, recorded in mythology and dismissed by history, but as real today as it was millennia ago.

"This also isn't Crete," Wayne added. "Mazes are everywhere. They're associated with death and the underworld in lots of cultures. Even the Holy Grail is supposed to be hidden in one. The real Labyrinth of Crete is in Knossos, I think. But the legend of that labyrinth could have started from one like this."

"Wow," said Nicole. She was thoroughly impressed.

Brandy grinned. "He's showing you up, Honey."

Albert laughed. "Good. Maybe he'll come in handy up ahead."

"Maybe I will." Wayne continued across the bridge, not looking at any of them. The others hesitated, still looking wonderingly down at the maze below.

Albert listened to the strange noise of the unseen hounds and wondered if they resembled bulls in any way. In his mind's eye he could almost see their oozing, fleshy snouts sniffing up at them, wicked horns carving the dry air as they turned. The thought gave him a shiver.

"Which way do we go?" Wayne asked as he stood before the three tunnels and the four statues.

"The one on the right," Albert replied, catching up to him. "Look." He shined his flashlight up at the sentinel's neck.

It was hard to see, but a close inspection revealed the

shape scratched into the stone.

"It looks like a bird. And there was a bird feather in my box."

"I see," Wayne said. "I hope there's enough tricks in that box of yours to get us through this place."

"Me too."

"Isn't this the tunnel that gets small?" Nicole asked.

Albert nodded. "Yeah. We'll have to go single file just a little ways down and then we'll have to crawl."

"Fun," Wayne remarked. He still wasn't entirely with them. His head was cloudy.

"Yeah," Albert agreed. "Who wants to go first?"

"Aw, hell, I will," Wayne volunteered. "I've been taking up the rear all night." He stepped into the tunnel and began to walk, not waiting for anyone to agree or object.

Albert turned to the girls and motioned at the tunnel. "Ladies first."

Brandy kissed him as she passed him by, a quick peck on the lips and a little smile. "*Merci.*" She was doing okay down here, he saw, probably feeling more secure with Wayne and Nicole along for the ride. He was surprised, however, that she had lost her modesty so quickly in front of Wayne. But then again, he had already begun to forget that he was naked in front of Nicole, and vice versa, it seemed.

Nicole went next and, taking a cue from Brandy, gave Albert a small peck on the cheek as she passed. "*Merci*," she repeated, grinning the same mischievous grin she always reserved for those moments when she knew she had succeeded in embarrassing him. She then hurried after Brandy, both of them giggling a little at his expense. Brandy and Nicole had both taken French in high school and in college, and Albert understood why Gomez Adams was always driven into a tizzy when Morticia spoke it.

Grinning a little in spite of everything, he stared after them for a moment before following them down the passage.

It did not take long for the tunnel to narrow to a claustrophobic size. Soon they were hunched over, then on their hands and knees. It was right about here, as he was crawling through the darkness and dragging his backpack beneath him, that Albert realized his mistake.

Thirteen months ago, when he and Brandy first came down this tunnel, he'd asked Brandy if she wanted to go first or last and she'd chosen first. When the two of them had to get down on their hands and knees to continue, he discovered a magnificent view of Brandy, a view that was not just intimate, but pornographic. Now, as he crawled through this tunnel again, he realized that he'd managed to get not behind his girlfriend, with whose body he was now familiar, but Nicole! Just a short distance from his face was her round, bare bottom and the sensual slit of her sex between her lean thighs. He looked right at this part of her and blushed hot and red at the sight, yet for a moment he was unable to take his eyes off of her.

Since that first night in these dark tunnels, he had seen Brandy's body literally hundreds of times. He thought back to their second date. To another couple it would have been too soon, too fast, but they'd been to the temple. They'd been to the sex room. In her bedroom at her parents' house, where she lived until she moved in with him just two months ago, immediately after one of their Chemistry lectures where they had already begun to do little more than stare at each other, the two of them lay together on her bed, kissing and holding and touching, their bodies filled with passion. He'd been burning for her since returning from the temple, and she had been burning as hot for him. They stripped off each other's clothes and made hot, passionate love together, then a second time soon after, slower and more tender.

Between their experiences in the sex room and the passionate lovemaking in the weeks to follow, it was a miracle that she had not gotten pregnant. It was a while before they even got around to taking the time to buy some condoms. They had merely done their best to be careful. After all, they'd never expected to keep feeling so much lust for each other. Since then, she'd gone on the pill, and even now Albert wondered sometimes if they weren't pressing their luck.

Albert thought of all those nights he spent making love to Brandy, of the time he spent just lying beside her and running his hands over her skin, relishing her warmth and smoothness. He had studied her body, admired every part of her, including that sacred place between her thighs. He had never been with anyone before her, had never looked upon this part of any other woman, and now that he saw this intimate part of Nicole, he found himself noticing the many differences between the two of them. Their hair was different, of course, but so was the size. Nicole was somewhat larger down there than Brandy, though equally as lovely.

He lowered his eyes and looked at the floor. His face was still burning and he felt guilty at having looked. Yet he could not help feeling a little privileged. Nicole was a beautiful woman, inside and out. He would consider any man who got to see that part of her lucky as hell.

But on the other hand, that image of her was now burned into his brain. He could not seem to force it out of his mind. Worse still, he did not *want* to force the image away.

Perhaps he could simply blame it on the sex room.

Up ahead, Brandy, too, had fixed her eyes on the floor. Ahead of her was Wayne, and from her vantage point, she had seen more of him than she'd bargained for. She remembered a similar view she had of Albert the last time she was in this tunnel, and found herself thinking about Albert and Nicole behind her. One part of her was glad that Nicole was not behind Albert, where she could see what she was now seeing of Wayne, but another part of her wondered what Albert was seeing right now. She wished that she had made Nicole go ahead of her. A wicked spike of jealousy rose in her heart and she felt almost ashamed to recognize it.

But even as she wished this, she found her eyes lifting, returning again to Wayne's body, examining his anatomy, noticing his size and the way gravity affected him, unable to resist her curiosity. She even found herself a little turned on by the sight, by the voyeuristic naughtiness of the view, just as she'd been all those months ago when she found herself studying Albert's body from the same vantage point. But she was less turned on this time. Although he was somewhat better endowed than her boyfriend—which was admittedly *interesting*—Wayne's posterior wasn't nearly as attractive as Albert's, in her opinion. It was considerably larger, for starters. And a little too hairy.

Besides, she didn't think this was any man's best angle, not even her beloved Albert's.

Ahead, Wayne had reached the sharp right turn and was awkwardly navigating around it. He wasn't as small as the rest of them and he was beginning to wonder if he'd make it all the way through.

"How narrow is this going to get?" Nicole asked. She stared at Brandy's feet as she crawled. She, too, had noticed what this tunnel revealed of her friend's body and wondered what Albert was seeing of her at this very moment. But she was surprised at how little embarrassment she felt at the idea. Perhaps the shock of being suddenly naked in his and Wayne's presence had obliterated most of her modesty. Or perhaps it was simply that she naturally felt comfortable in Albert's presence. She certainly felt that they were very good friends, after all. Either way, it was refreshing that she was able to feel such freedom in a place like this. It was one less discomfort she would have to face.

Albert now stared only at the floor as he crawled across the smooth stone, trying hard not to raise his eyes in front of him. "Pretty narrow," he replied.

The four of them made the right turn and started down the last stretch of tunnel. Soon they were on their bellies and, as lovely as she was, Albert was relieved to no longer have Nicole's bottom in his face.

“I think I see the end,” Wayne reported, grunting, “but I’m not sure I’m going to make it.”

“You’re going to have to,” Albert said.

“I’m going to try, but I ain’t promising anything.”

Their bellies were on the cold, hard surface of the floor, the ceiling of the tunnel slowly closing down on their backs.

“I don’t like this!” Nicole said, her voice quivering a little with her growing claustrophobia.

“We can get through,” promised Brandy. “Just keep going.”

Wayne could see the tunnel’s opening just a few feet ahead, but his shoulders were already pushing against the closing walls. The ceiling was only an inch or two off his back. He turned himself slightly so that his shoulders spanned the tunnel diagonally, where it was the widest, and pushed. The surfaces in here were very smooth, almost slippery, and he could not get enough of a grip to push himself forward.

“Come on, Wayne,” Brandy urged. “You’re almost there.”

“I really don’t like this,” Nicole said again.

"You'll do fine," Brandy insisted. "You're skinnier than me and I made it through here."

"Well my tits are bigger," Nicole retorted. "That means I have less room to breathe."

"Well aren't you special!" Brandy snapped back.

Just a few more inches and he might be able to reach the exit and use it as a handhold, but Wayne's momentum was nearly stopped. He tried to take a deep breath of air and found that he couldn't. The walls had closed in around him until he was wedged against the stone. Claustrophobia washed over him like icy water, threatening to drown him. "*Oh god*!"

"It's okay!" Brandy promised. She could not reach his hand, so she grabbed his ankle and gave it a reassuring squeeze. "Just relax."

"Yeah," Wayne said. "Relax." He closed his eyes and concentrated. He fought back the things that were making him panic, the lack of space and air, but it was a losing battle.

"Come on, Wayne," Nicole urged from farther back. He could hear the concern rising in her voice. She didn't want to be stuck down here. She was scared. Panic was just around the corner.

Wayne could feel himself losing. Soon he would panic and then probably get hopelessly lodged in this tight space. They would not be able to get past him. They'd have to backtrack. They'd have to leave him here!

Suddenly, and for reasons he could not explain, he thought of Laura Swiff.

He focused his thoughts on her, on his encounter with her that morning, on those sexy, muddy eyes. He had wanted only to forget her, to stop thinking about her seductive advances, yet in the light of being lodged in this tunnel, of his fear of suffocating here in this tiny corridor, her lecherous advances seemed like such a ridiculous thing to obsess over. In fact, it was a welcome thought. He did not just *remember* her not-so-subtle proposition, he *reconsidered* it. Maybe when he got out of here he'd take care of that business. He'd already managed to give her the impression that he might be interested. She was certain to make herself accessible to him again in the near future. She wanted him, after all.

Wayne lay there silently for a moment, thinking about Laura Swiff and all the things he would do to her when he got home, all the things he would do to forget Beverly Bridger and Olivia Shadey and all the rest of the unpleasantness he had found since leaving her alone and unsatisfied in his empty apartment.

"Wayne?" Brandy's voice, a little concerned. "Are you okay?"

"What's wrong?" Nicole asked. There was an edge to her voice that suggested tears would not be far off.

"Wayne?" Brandy squeezed his ankle.

"I'm fine," Wayne assured them. His body was finally relaxing, his tension flowing out of him in great waves. "Just thinking." He lay there for a moment longer, imagining what Laura might look like naked, perhaps perched on top of him as he lay on his back, her body rising and falling in a soft, flowing motion, her muddy eyes filled with lust and gazing down at him.

"Well think faster!" Nicole hissed.

He could move. And in just a few seconds he had pushed himself far enough to grab hold of the ledge, but he found that he did not need it. He pushed with his feet until his shoulders were free of the tunnel and then pushed himself out with his arms and tumbled onto the hard floor, cursing at the painful landing.

Brandy, Nicole and Albert followed him out of the tunnel, each of them not so much exiting as spilling onto the floor.

"We made it," Albert sighed, and thought to himself that the real trick would be going back the other way. He looked back and saw that the two lipstick Xs Brandy used to mark the passage the first time they came here were still clearly visible.

Wayne stretched, glad to be free of that place, and immediately shoved his mental image of Laura Swiff to the back of his mind, knowing somehow that she would not stay there. He stood in a huge, round room. There were many more openings identical to the one he'd just tumbled from, openings that led to God only knew where. The one from which they exited was still marked with Brandy's lipstick from their previous visit. In the center of this room was the widest, deepest hole he'd ever seen. A single sentinel stood pointing down a spiraling stone staircase. "Wow," he said, hardly believing what he was seeing.

Albert peered down into the hole. "The fear room's

at the bottom of these steps," he informed everyone. "We're getting closer. Be careful. There's no railing and it's a long way down."

The four of them began to descend the narrow, stone stairs, growing ever closer to the room that had proven to be the limit of Albert and Brandy's courage. What lay beyond that terrible room, no one knew except perhaps the blind man, and so far he had not told.

Chapter 11

After he had walked for a while, Wayne began to think of Laura again, as he knew he eventually would. He was taking up the rear again, his eyes fixed on his feet as he carefully descended into this strange oblivion of darkness. He knew he should not let this trouble with Laura bother him so much. If he wanted to fuck her he should just fuck her and if he didn't he should just tell her to piss off and forget about it. But it wasn't as simple as that. He didn't know why, but he just couldn't let it go. The truth was that he wanted to do it. He was only twenty-two, without a real care in the world. Nothing tied him down. There was no reason to let something like this dominate his thoughts. He had told himself that the only reason he didn't want to go through with it was that she was Charlie's girlfriend, but he'd since discovered the truth about Charlie. And yet the wrongness of it still gnawed at him, struggling against that other part of him, the part that wanted the soft feel of a woman's arms again…even if that woman happened to be a vulgar whore.

He felt a wave of anger flow through him, but it was weak, tired. Besides, he was not angry with Laura. He was not angry with Charlie, either. He was angry with himself. This was all about Wayne. This was about issues that went back way before he ever met Charlie or Laura.

He looked down at the three people descending the steps ahead of him and realized for the first time that they were probably as close as he'd been to having real friends in a very long time. All his buddies from high school were gone. Mark and Sam were attending the University of Missouri in St. Louis, Brent was off on the east coast somewhere practicing his salute for Uncle Sam, Will… well God only knew where the hell Will was. He disappeared shortly after graduation. And Harvey got married almost right out of high school and went to work for some construction company. He hadn't heard from any of them more than a few times since sophomore year, and he was a senior now. There was something like a spark in his head as he realized this, a new light where there wasn't one before, like a star being born in his conscious mind. Suddenly it all began to make a little more sense. He wasn't obsessing over Laura Swiff. He never was. He was obsessing over himself.

He sat down, feeling a little dazed. He supposed it took watching two people die and him getting his fat ass lodged in a narrow tunnel to bring it close enough to the surface for him to actually see it. He wanted to sleep with Laura simply because he wanted to be with someone. He was lonely. He'd known this all along, after all, but he hadn't realized just how lonesome he'd become. His roommate was always telling him he should get out more, go to a party, hit a football game, something. He'd always figured that Charlie just liked to tell him how to run his life, but he'd actually had a point. When was the last time he went out? When was the last time he had any real fun? He hadn't been with a girl since Gail Porbin, his high school girlfriend, with whom he'd broken up shortly after graduation. He wanted the companionship that he sorely missed after Gail was gone. But he did not want a one-night stand and these were the words that Laura Swiff probably had tattooed on her ass.

The others walked on for little ways before noticing that Wayne had stopped. When they did, they paused and looked back, concerned.

"Wayne?" Albert asked. "You okay, buddy?"

Buddy. That was what Charlie called him. Buddy. Not that Charlie really was his buddy, though. He never had been. Not really. They were just two guys who happened to usually get along. "Yeah. Just…reality check, I guess."

Nicole was closest to him. She turned and climbed back up the steps to where he sat. "What's up?"

Wayne shook his head. "Too much at once."

"Are you okay?"

"Yeah. I just need to rest here a minute, get my thoughts together."

Nicole sat down in front of him, her lovely eyes fixed fretfully on him. She had crossed her arms over her chest again, but it was a half-hearted effort. Hiding herself just didn't seem important by now. After this long, what was the point?

Albert and Brandy sat down and listened. Albert was strongly reminded of the last time they were here. They'd stopped to rest on these steps as well, both on the way up and on the way down, and both times they'd talked. This was where they'd gotten to know each other a little better. And this was where they were going to get to know Wayne a little better, too.

"I'm sorry I was hard on Beverly back there," Wayne said. "I'm usually not a mean person. At least, I don't try to be."

Nicole shook her head. "Don't worry about that."

"I *do* worry about it. I don't have a friend in this world. I watched two people die today." He lifted his face and looked into Nicole's lovely eyes. "This morning, I almost screwed my roommate's girlfriend."

With several comical blinks, Nicole's eyes stuttered from sweet sympathy to startled surprise. "Um… Wait. *What*?"

"Yeah. *Almost*. I don't even like her. She's a pig. A foul-mouthed little slut, to be blunt. She's trying to seduce me and this morning I almost let her." He looked back down at his feet again. "That's what I'm doing here, actually. I had to get away, do some thinking, get my mind off things. I figured I'd check out Gilbert House; find out why someone was willing to pay a thousand bucks to get me to go inside it." He looked around him, at the enormous, spiraling staircase that vanished into darkness above and below him. "Never bargained for this, though."

Nicole put a hand on his knee. "It doesn't sound to me like you did anything wrong."

Wayne smiled at her. She was sweet. But she didn't know just how much he had done wrong. He thought about Gail. Sweet Gail. Beautiful Gail. He couldn't remember the last time he let himself think of her.

"Can you go on?" Albert asked. "Because if you can't—"

"I can. I just…" Wayne shook his head. "Like I said before. Reality check. Everything just came crashing in all at once."

"It'll probably take a while before it all completely sets in," Nicole offered. "For all of us. I mean, none of us are used to seeing people die. I know *I'm* still feeling kind of numb from it all."

"*I* just keep thinking of you guys," Brandy said. "I can't stop and have a breakdown if I still have the three of you to look after."

Albert gave her a smile and squeezed her hand. That certainly sounded like the Brandy he'd come to know and adore. "I think I became a little numb to it all when I met that thing in Gilbert House. I feel like, even after what happened to Olivia and Beverly, we've actually been pretty lucky so far. At least the rest of us are still here. And there'll be time to think about them when this is all over and we're back in our own homes."

Nicole nodded, smiling a little.

Wayne sat there for a moment longer, thinking. Then he stood up, ready to move on. "Sorry, guys."

"Don't be sorry," Brandy said.

"Yeah," agreed Nicole as she gazed up at him from her place on the steps. "I think we all needed to stop and take a second."

She stood up and the four of them continued down the steps.

Wayne's thoughts again drifted to Laura Swiff and he found that he was not as tempted by her lechery as he had been before. It seemed almost funny now, really. He wondered what she was doing at that very moment, but then he decided he really did not care. Instead, he thought about Gail again. For the first time in a very long time, he wondered what *she* was doing.

Chapter 12

An anxious feeling fell over the group as they walked across the chamber at the bottom of the steps. It was an enormous space, stretching into the darkness all around them. Its emptiness was almost overwhelming, and each step they took made them feel smaller and smaller.

Albert was eager, almost twitching with anticipation. The answers to all the questions he had about the Temple of the Blind must lie on the other side of this obstacle, waiting for him just beyond. And yet he also felt like a prisoner being taken to the torture chamber one last time before being set free. The fear room was not like the sex room. It was not like the hate room. The dangers there were much more real, much more extravagant.

Brandy felt none of Albert's eagerness. The things she'd seen in the fear room had given her nightmares for weeks. In the sex room, the images had driven them to act upon sexual impulses they'd hardly known were there, but the images themselves had conveyed no real meaning other than the obvious allusions to desire and lust. The statues in the fear room were different. When she'd seen them, even without her glasses, they had reminded her of things she'd never actually known, but things that she somehow knew to be real, things from a past she'd never lived.

She wasn't sure whether she believed that these memories were real or not. The logical part of her insisted that they could not possibly be real, that they were merely subliminal messages of some kind, cleverly designed to trick her brain into believing these terrible things to be true. Surely they could not be actual events, somehow carried to her through those statues. But they were so vivid, so *convincing*.

Albert gazed up into the shadows of the high ceiling above them as he walked. This room felt like the one that had killed Beverly, and the emptiness made him nervous.

What happened back there, he wondered. What did Beverly see when she stepped into that room? Whatever it was had been so terrible that she had forgotten the real danger behind her.

Again he thought he heard a distant sound, like chains rattling somewhere very far away, yet the very sound was like a memory, gone before it was recognized, almost before it began.

Ahead of them, a great stone wall appeared, and with it the doorway to the entrance of the fear room.

Nicole felt a knot growing in her stomach. She knew what awaited her ahead, and she wasn't sure if she had what it was going to take to get to the other side. So far, everything Albert and Brandy told her had been completely true. Every detail was just as they'd described. If anything, it *surpassed* her imagination.

They passed through the doorway and walked between the first pair of statues without pausing.

"Who's going first this time?" Nicole asked as she watched the silent warning the sentinels acted out on both sides of the room. It really was like frames in a cartoon.

After a while, they began to feel like a single statue actually moving from one pose to the next.

"This one's worse than the others," Albert warned. "The fact that it's the fear room is enough to make you nervous. You start off frightened. And once you're a little bit scared, it only escalates. Before long you're in a panic. And we have to remember what was waiting after the hate room for people who lose control."

Wayne wondered if he'd ever be able to forget it. He watched the sentinels as they lifted their arms and sank to the floor, their freakish hands splayed before them, shielding their featureless faces from some unseen horror. It was eerily reminiscent of Beverly's reaction to that empty room. "Is there another of those spike traps in here?"

"I don't know," Albert replied.

"We never made it through last time," Brandy explained.

"If I were to guess," Albert added, "I'd say there's probably going to be *something* nasty in there somewhere." On either side of them, the sentinels arched their backs and lifted their blank faces in silent screams of unthinkable terror. "It'll probably be something a lot worse than a spiked pit."

Ahead of them, the door appeared. It was the same as the last time Albert laid eyes on it, a woman with a round, almost pudgy face and a mole under her right eye. The scream in which she was frozen was so fierce, so strained, that it seemed she should fly apart. Her eyes bulged with fright, her lips peeled back in terrible panic. It was easy for Nicole and Wayne to see why Albert and Brandy spoke so fearfully of this place. If this was just the door, then what must wait inside?

"We'll probably have to trade off," Albert reasoned as they approached the insanely terrified face. "I'll go first. Then Brandy?" He looked at her and she nodded agreement. "Then Nicole." He looked back at Wayne. "You can be last. When we feel like we can't take it anymore, we'll pass off. Hopefully by the time you can't go on, I'll be recharged and we can start over again."

"Hopefully it won't take that long," whimpered Brandy.

Wayne nodded.

Albert held his hand out for Brandy's glasses. "We

might as well get started. Is everybody ready?"

Everybody was.

He made it his business to hurry. As soon as he stepped into the fear room, Albert headed straight into the jungle of gray shapes, determined to make the most of his turn. All around him, dark shapes appeared and melted. Shades of gray shifted and faded, merging and dividing. It was dizzying, and after just a few steps, he had to pause to focus himself.

Each of these emotion rooms was larger than the last, with more statues than the last. Each became more difficult to navigate. This one was a virtual maze of stone figures. There was hardly room to walk. Navigating with such dim vision was nearly impossible. No wonder Brandy had gotten lost in here.

In front of him, several forms came together and each one seemed unnervingly familiar to him, as though he'd seen it in some long forgotten nightmare. They were like bogeymen from past lives, each one very different but no less frightening than the next.

"Are you okay?" Brandy asked.

"Yeah," Albert replied, but he wasn't sure how much

longer he'd remain okay. This room was a scene straight from hell. Even mostly blind he could see that the things in this room were not someone's idea of scary Halloween ghosts and goblins. These were things so real, so terrible, only the insane or immortal could have captured them in stone. If these horrors weren't real, then they were designed to make them *believe* that they were real and that was just as bad.

He went left, then right, and then he had to stop. To his right was something that made him think of sand and screaming, to his left was a vague silhouette of a woman he had a feeling was in the process of dying. A deep uneasiness had settled into him and it was beginning to take root and grow, like a cancer slowly eating away his courage. He wanted to look around the glasses, to take just a quick peek and make sure there was nothing there, staring at him from the shadows, waiting to pounce. But he could not allow himself to do that. He had to remain strong. It was all about willpower over fear.

He tried to clear his mind, blocking out as much distraction as he could, and kept walking. He picked out landmarks to follow, statues that could be spotted from a distance, and then focused his eyes on an imaginary point just to one side of it, trying hard to not look directly at any of the shapes. He thought not about the statues, but about the traps. There must be at least one in or beyond this room, a spiked pit or a sleeping hound or some other unthinkable device.

He squeezed his eyes into small slits and focused fiercely on looking only straight ahead. Soon his head began to ache, but he couldn't risk letting himself glimpse the horrors that oozed in around the lenses.

He might have gone in circles two or three times trying to gain his bearings. He was beginning to think that he'd gotten them all hopelessly lost in this funhouse from hell, but then he spotted the silhouette of a tall figure, a sentinel, with arms outstretched. It seemed almost to be beckoning him. Was this the way out? He remembered Brandy mentioning that she'd seen a sentinel statue in the first chamber of the fear room. She'd found it curious at the time and now he did too. It seemed to defeat the purpose somehow. He'd begun to think of these deformed and faceless men as symbols of the temple's honesty. They were always at guard where a dangerous decision was required, even though they refused to help. There were not any sentinels inside the sex room. There hadn't been one to warn them of the spiked pit, either. Those were trials that they'd been forced to conquer on their own. So why would one be standing here inside the fear room?

But he was in no mood to complain.

He turned toward the sentinel, focusing on it. He almost peeked over the glasses at it, curious about its presence in this room, but he reminded himself that it was surrounded by horrors that he could not allow himself to look upon.

As he approached this sentinel and passed it, he saw the square opening up ahead. "I see the door," he announced. "It leads into another chamber. How is everybody?"

"I'm fine," Nicole replied.

"I'm okay," Brandy assured him.

"No problem," Wayne chimed in. He sounded almost cheerful. Albert guessed that he was trying to keep himself psyched up for his turn.

Nicole made a sudden hissing noise through her teeth

and Albert stopped, startled. “What happened?”

“Something cut me,” she said. “My leg.”

“The statue!” Brandy exclaimed. “That thing cut me last time I was here, too! I forgot all about it.”

Albert remembered. “That’s right. It got me too. On the way out. It’s got a claw or something. Are you okay?”

“Yeah. It just stings. Be careful.”

Albert stepped into the next room and paused. His eyes fell upon the statue directly in front of him, and although he couldn’t see it, he already knew what it looked like. His mind produced a perfect image of what he had seen all those months ago, every detail as perfect as if he had taken Brandy’s glasses off his face and boldly stared at it.

The woman’s face was particularly vivid.

Oh, God! he thought, with inexplicable horror. *That poor woman!* He could see nothing but shades of gray, yet he could see the blood and the pain and the madness and the cruelty. Why were they doing that? Why were they forcing her into that hole? What had she done to deserve such an end? How could they continue doing that to her with her screaming (*begging*) like that?

"Albert?" Brandy's voice was frightened.

She begged them. She pleaded with them to stop. She promised them anything they wanted, her money, her body, her *soul*, and still they dragged her down into the deepest chambers of those awful catacombs with a glee that was actually *sexual* in its intensity.

"Albert? Are you okay?"

Albert shook away the image. "Yeah. Just…bad stuff in here."

Brandy did not reply. Her eyes were tightly closed, her heart pounding. She prayed that he would just start moving again. She knew what he had seen. She could almost see that horrible statue too, even with her eyes firmly closed.

Albert began to walk again, turning his eyes away from that awful statue, but unable to tear his mind from it. *They were her friends*, he thought suddenly, and although he didn't understand how he knew this, he did not doubt that it was true. *They were her friends and they had sex after they shoved her in. All three of them had sex while they listened to her dying screams.*

He walked on, trying hard to force these images from

his head. This chamber was slightly less crowded than the first one, but still it was difficult to navigate, especially when his head was filled with the terrible screaming of a dead woman.

Brandy held his hand and followed close behind him. "Stop when you need to," she reminded him. "I can take my turn whenever you're ready."

"I know," Albert replied. "I'm okay." And he *was* still okay. He just had to focus on where he was going and not on what was around him. They were just statues, after all, just reminders of bad things, things that might not even exist. As long as he kept his eyes forward, away from the edges of Brandy's glasses…

But that was so hard. His fear made him want to look, to make sure nothing was lurking among the statues around him. Just a little peek. A mere second. Half a second. Just to be sure there was nothing there. He had to keep telling himself that the fear he imagined was far better than the fear that he would experience if he dared to take that peek.

"Don't overdo it," Nicole pleaded.

"Yeah," agreed Wayne. "If you overdo it, you might

not recover to take over for me."

That was a good point, Albert realized. If he waited until he physically couldn't go any farther, he might not have the courage to put the glasses back on if it came back to him. For that matter, he might be too afraid to carry on even with his eyes closed. Wasn't that exactly what happened to Brandy last time? "Just a little farther," he promised. "Then Brandy can take over."

"Right," agreed Brandy, although she didn't sound very enthused to Albert. He didn't blame her. She suffered quite a scare last time she was here.

He made his way around another statue, still narrowing his eyes to keep them behind the small lenses.

He almost walked right into it. He was clearing his head, focusing his attention on the task at hand, when he glimpsed the thing that was sticking toward him. It wasn't any part of a human. It was long and thin. Perhaps it was part of some odd creature, like the thing that was killing the woman in that awful statue that greeted him when he entered this room. He bent toward it, examining it, and when it finally dawned on him what it was, he suddenly felt as if his stomach was filled with ice water.

"Oh shit," he breathed. Panic welled up inside him, threatening to overwhelm him.

"What?" Brandy asked, alarmed. "What is it?"

Albert had wondered what could make the fear room more deadly than the hate room with its spiked pit. Now he knew. And now that he knew, he was terrified to even move.

"Albert?"

"Spikes," he replied. "Coming up from the floor. Don't anybody move." He tried to focus his eyes on what was around him. He could see a few sticking out from the wall now that he was looking for them.

"Like the ones Beverly fell on?" Nicole asked.

"Yeah. But more of them. They're coming up from the floor at an angle. On the walls, too." Albert could not see well enough with Brandy's glasses on to spot them all, yet if he took them off he would surely panic at the sight of the statues that stood around him. If he panicked, he could run himself right through, which was exactly the reasoning behind these horrible things, he was sure.

"Okay. We have to take our time in here. If we don't, if we let ourselves get scared and we start to hurry, one or more of us will wind up just like Beverly, but vertical." It was a horrible image, but hopefully it would prove to drive home the point…or not, as the case may be.

"Well then let's all just remain calm," Wayne said. "How're you doing?"

Albert steeled himself mentally. "I'm holding in there." He began to walk forward, moving slowly, with deliberate cautiousness. He focused on watching for the spikes and found them to be an easier fear to deal with than the mysterious statues. He reminded himself that as long as he kept his pace slow, those giant needles could give only an annoying poke. And with Brandy's glasses on, his eyes would be protected. "Stay right behind me. Try not to veer to the sides."

His pride also helped to hold back the fear, he found. He *wanted* to be brave. He didn't want to look like a coward, no matter how justified his fear may be. It was not so much for Brandy, who knew the horrors of this room as well as he did, or even for Nicole. Ironically, it was a childish, petty urge to prove that he was braver than bigger, stronger Wayne, who had now seen his girlfriend naked. It was silly, to say the least, but it helped a little, so he embraced it.

This second chamber of the fear room was curved. It wrapped around the first, circling to the right. The statues were many, but not as many as there had been before, and these were somehow not as bad. Most were formless, hunched shadows or vague, human shapes, with no real meaning to his handicapped eyes. Only one caught his attention: an unusually tall and slim figure far to his right.

It was not a man or a woman, but something else, something not human, but upright, just the same. As his eyes swept across this, he thought for some reason about fog. *Dense* fog. Fog so thick that he could barely see his own hand. There was something terribly creepy about this image, something incredibly unsettling. (*They're everywhere!*) He turned away from the tall thing and the image of the fog became a hazy memory, but the eeriness it had instilled remained.

God, it was hard not to hurry.

"Is everyone still okay back there?" Albert asked, trying to focus his attention away from that strange eeriness. This room was like that fog, thick and gray and full of nasty, hiding surprises.

Brandy had let go of his hand and was holding onto his waist, her flashlight still in one clenched fist. She pressed her face against his backpack and said, "I'm okay."

"I'm fine, too." Nicole had her free hand on Brandy's shoulder.

"Me too," Wayne reported. "We're all fine. Just take care of yourself up there."

"You've already gotten farther than we got before," Brandy told him.

"I know," Albert said. He was moving toward the end of the room. Ahead he could just see the square outline of the door. "We're almost through this room."

"How many are there?" Nicole asked.

"I don't know," Albert confessed. "Could be just these two. Could be a hundred. Down here I don't doubt anything."

In the corner of the room, to the left of the door, there was a statue of a man with his arms outstretched. For just a moment something surfaced in Albert's mind, something (*he won't die!*) every bit as eerie as the image of the fog, but much more distant, much more vague. He focused on the doorway itself. He could see more of those narrow spikes jutting up from the floor on either side of it, angled inward. "Be careful going through the door. Follow me as close as you can or you'll get cut."

He stepped up to the doorway, but paused before entering it. "I'm going to try and see if this is the way out."

Brandy squeezed his waist, afraid for him.

Albert closed his eyes and removed the glasses. He then lowered his head so that he would be looking only at his feet when he opened his eyes. For a moment he stood that way, steeling himself for the fright he would likely see, wondering if there were things down here that could frighten a man so badly he could drop dead at the very sight. A childish paranoia ran through him, a horrible urge to quickly look around and make sure they were really alone, and he had to bite his lip to hold it back. At last, he lifted the hand he held Brandy's glasses in as if to shield himself from sunlight, and opened his eyes. He stared down at his own bare feet on solid stone. He held his eyes there, willing them not to move, then lifted them slowly, raising his hand as he did so, using it as a visor.

There was no pit of spikes, no trap of any other sort, but as he lifted his head, he saw a stone foot.

More statues.

Another chamber.

He closed his eyes immediately and returned Brandy's narrow glasses to his face. When he opened his eyes again, he found that could make out a large, awkward form standing in front of him. It was not shaped like a man, but more like three, huddled strangely close together. Looking at it sent an odd tingle up his spine.

More shapeless forms loomed behind this statue. "It's a third chamber," he reported. "Come on. Be careful."

As he walked past the first statue in this third chamber, his eyes fixed on the empty darkness ahead of him, he suddenly felt a piercing pain in his right arm. He drew back, hissing a little.

"What happened?" Brandy's voice was tinged with panic.

"Spike," he replied as he gazed down at the long, almost invisible thing that was jutting out from the statue. "Some of them are sticking out of the statues. Watch yourselves."

Brandy was not concerned with herself. "Are you okay?"

Albert assured her that he was and continued walking, his left hand pressed against a shallow, bleeding gash in his right arm, just below the elbow.

The statues in this third chamber were in greater numbers than in the second, but were not so many as were in the first. As he walked, he saw that there was another doorway immediately ahead and to the left, behind a large, animal-like statue. "I think I see the next door." The room continued on past this doorway, curving toward the right as the last one had, and he wondered, not for the first time, if one of these rooms could have more than one exit.

"Already?" Nicole sounded skeptical.

"It seems sort of random," Albert explained, "sort of like a maze, hard to navigate, especially blind." As he approached this new door, he found the statue that stood between it and him disturbing. It reminded him of a forest somehow, thick and lush, almost a jungle. As he grew closer he imagined a noise, like the chirping of a squirrel, but louder, lower, more menacing. A feeling of overwhelming panic was welling up inside him and he had to stop and close his eyes. His every instinct told him to run, to hide, to just get the hell out of there before… Before what? He had closed his eyes, had blocked out the sight of that horrible statue, but still that feeling of impending doom remained.

"Albert?" Brandy's voice again, trembling, fearful.

Albert focused his thoughts on her, on keeping her safe. He stood there, silent and still, trying hard to focus on something other than the fear, on something other than this damned room. Why the hell had he wanted to come back here so badly? Nothing was worth this. Nothing.

"Albert?" Brandy again, the fear in her voice sharper than before.

"Albert?" Nicole's voice this time, sounding equally concerned.

"Okay," Albert tried to assure them, but his voice was soft and dry, almost inaudible. He took a deep breath, then another. "Okay," he said again, this time loud enough to be heard over the pounding of his heart. He took a third deep breath, held it, and then opened his eyes.

It came up from his right, lunging out of the darkness. In the space of a heartbeat, everything was blood and chaos. Something sharp entered low on his right side and jolted up and back, severing his spine with the speed and power of a machine. He screamed and fell to the floor, his lower body seemingly gone from beneath him.

"*Albert*!" Terrified, Brandy fell onto him, clutching him in her arms. Her eyes had flown open, but she saw only Albert, his limp form lying sprawled beneath her. "*Oh god!*"

Nicole, too, had opened her eyes when Albert screamed, and instantly she wished she hadn't. She was looking right into a great, snarling face, a beast with more teeth than head, covered with a thick, gray coat of stone fur. She staggered backward, into Wayne, and dropped her flashlight onto the floor. Then a huge arm wrapped around her waist and a thick hand fell over her eyes. She screamed out, terrified, kicking frantically.

"Calm down!" Wayne yelled. "Just calm down! I've got you! It's okay!"

Brandy was screaming Albert's name. She didn't understand what happened.

Albert felt light, like a balloon. The world around him was slowly spinning and seemed to be drifting away from him.

Brandy ran her hands over him, sliding them down to where he'd been speared, trying to understand what had happened. She was crying, terrified. "*Oh God!*" she cried. "*Oh God! Oh God! Oh God!*"

But she seemed so far away to Albert. Her touch didn't hurt. In fact, he could not feel her touch at all once her hands fell below the middle of his waist. He was numb down there, completely without feeling. Darkness grew around him, slowly swallowing him into its black belly, and he felt deep sleep beckoning him.

Nicole's kicking grew less frantic as she realized who it was that was holding her, and she began to wilt, embracing Wayne's big, comforting arms. *This isn't happening*, she thought as her best friend begged God for some kind of miracle. *Please say this isn't happening.*

Wayne had not opened his eyes when Albert screamed. He froze in place, squeezing his eyes tightly closed. If asked, he could not have said why or how. Perhaps it was the thought of those random spikes sticking out from the statues and walls all around him, ready to impale anyone who panicked in these dark rooms, or perhaps he had just gotten lucky and froze in pure fright. Either way, he'd managed to remain in control throughout the chaos that had suddenly erupted around him. Now he stood, clutching Nicole against him, still holding his hand over her eyes as he listened to the drama that was unfolding before him.

Brandy didn't understand. The confusion was almost a physical thing, dark and slippery. She took Albert's hand, but it was weak. She called his name, but he did not answer.

Albert slowly faded, sinking toward a darkness that was deeper than any sleep.

Brandy fell over him, holding him in her arms. "*Albert…*" she begged, sobbing. "*Albert…no…*"

Chapter 13

"Albert…" Brandy's voice was soft and pitiful. She didn't understand. How could it have come to this? "Please, Albert…"

Nicole's heart shattered as she listened to this. "Albert…?" she whispered. "Is he…?" She did not want to say it, did not want to hear the answer.

Tears rolled down Brandy's face. This wasn't right. This wasn't how it was supposed to be. They could lose Olivia and Beverly, but Albert was the one who was supposed to get the rest of them through this thing. It was *his* adventure. It *started* with him. He was the one who solved the riddles of the box.

Why did she come back down here? What could be

worth risking this? They never should have pressed their luck after returning from Gilbert House. They should've just gone home and stayed there. The phones couldn't ring forever, could they? She took a long, shuddering breath. What were they going to do now? How would they go on? How would *she* go on?

"Brandy?" It was Wayne who spoke, his voice commanding in the silence, yet gentle. When she did not reply, he spoke again: "Brandy. What happened?"

"Nothing." This was Albert's voice, spoken as he spiraled back from his strange plummet into darkness.

Brandy let out a great, wet sob and squeezed him, so thankful to hear his voice again. Her heart was thudding with such relief that she thought it might explode in her chest.

Nicole made a sound as if someone socked her in the belly, a whoop of expelled air mixed with a great sob of relief. Wayne could feel her tears against the palm of his hand.

"What the fuck?" Wayne asked.

"I don't know," Albert confessed. He sat up, wrapping his arms around Brandy as she sobbed against him. Keeping his eyes closed was no real task. He felt as though he'd just awakened from a deep sleep, his lids heavy. He ran one hand down his right side. There was no blood, no wound, no numbness in his legs. He was fine. Nothing had touched him. It was all just a vivid memory, a terrible hallucination.

"*You don't know*?" Wayne exclaimed. "Hell, I thought you *died* or something!"

"So did I," Albert said and held Brandy a little tighter. "The statues in here are *real* bad. I shouldn't have led for so long."

"Give me the glasses," Wayne said. He dropped his hand from over Nicole's eyes and released his grip on her waist. She lingered for only a moment, orienting herself, and then felt her way to Albert and Brandy, following the sound of her best friend's weeping. "I'll take my turn next. I think the girls have had all the trauma they can take for a little while."

"Okay." Albert didn't have the energy to argue, even if he wanted. He was still trembling. Somewhere, in some other time very distant from now, someone once experienced that very same death. Only that person never returned from the darkness. He'd somehow taken that memory from the statue, just as he'd picked up the vague images of the forest before that. As he sat there, he wondered again if this knowledge could possibly be real, or if the statues only made him believe them to be real. He supposed it didn't matter. Either way, it was effective.

For a moment they all remained where they were, letting the shock of the chaos fade away, letting the world slow to its normal speed again. Albert held Brandy. Brandy held Albert. Nicole held them both, kneeling over them like their guardian angel.

In the intimate silence, Wayne stood patiently, listening and waiting, giving them the moment that they needed.

At last, Albert stood up. Brandy and Nicole still clung to him, both of them reluctant to let him go. He reached out, blindly, and handed Brandy's glasses to Wayne. "The door's over there," he said, "straight in front of you. Try not to look at the statue in front of it. You won't like what you see."

"I don't expect I would." Wayne slipped Brandy's glasses onto his face. On him, they looked even more comical than they had on Albert, like a set of granny bifocals, dwarfed by his large, round face, but no one was looking at him anyway. He could see the square opening directly ahead of him. He could also see the statue in front of that opening, and he felt a strange uneasiness at the sight of it.

Wayne closed his eyes for a moment, preparing himself for what he was about to do. The feeling of uneasiness he felt from the formless statue did not vanish with his sight. It lingered like the smell of a recently removed carcass.

He thought about Beverly, called upon the memory of her lying in the pit, the tips of those terrible spikes protruding from her pale skin. He tried to imagine what she might have felt in those final seconds. Did she feel every agonizing pierce as the giant needles were driven up into her naked body? It was a terribly morbid thought, but it served to focus his attention on what was important. He did not intend to let anyone else die today.

When he opened his eyes, he focused not on the statue, but on the thin, stone thorns that surrounded the door behind it. He would have to keep his head if he was going to get them through this.

“Everybody ready?” he asked.

“As ready as we’re going to get,” Albert replied. He was standing behind Wayne. Both Brandy and Nicole were still pressed against him, the three of them huddled together in an intimate group hug. He felt horrible about his strange delusion. He had terrified them, not merely startling them when he cried out, but actually making them believe something had killed him. He could not even imagine how it would have felt if it had been Brandy lying there, apparently slipping away from him.

“I love you so much!” Brandy wept, her voice muffled against his skin.

“I love you too,” Albert assured her. “Come on. Let’s get moving. I don’t want to be here anymore.”

As she pulled away, Nicole slapped him softly on his chest. “I swear to God,” she said, her voice trembling, “if you ever die for real I’ll kill myself and come kick your fucking ass!”

Albert smiled. “You do that.” He pulled them both to him once more, holding them for another moment.

Wayne felt a cold and lonely pang of jealousy.

Albert was a very lucky man. He was really cared about, really loved. He stared ahead, still trying to focus on the memory of Beverly Bridger's body and not see the terrible statue in front of him. "The door's surrounded by those spikes," he said, trying to stay on track. "We'll go through slow. Stay as low as you can."

Albert and Nicole picked up their dropped flashlights and then began to move, Albert in back, Brandy ahead of him, Nicole ahead of her.

With his thoughts focused, Wayne had little trouble navigating around the statue.

"Don't go through the door without looking," Albert warned. "Remember the hate room."

Wayne stood in the doorway, startled by the thought. "How should I do that, exactly?"

"Use your hand to shield your eyes and check the floor. Try to see as little as possible. If there are more statues, close your eyes and put the glasses back on."

Wayne did as Albert said. The next room was a fourth chamber.

As he stepped through the door, looking at it through Brandy's eyes, he saw that many more spikes protruded from the clustered statues, threatening to pierce the flesh and organs of anyone foolish enough to get careless.

He took a deep breath, warned the others of the situation and then began to weave his way through the many statues.

Time slowed to a crawl as his eyes picked out shapes that reminded him of things he'd rather not see, things that made him want to break and run, to just get the hell out of there. But of course that would be committing suicide. He walked slowly, deliberately meticulous, gently prodding the darkness with his toes with every step he took and holding his hands before him to guard against unseen spikes. To be this afraid and not be able to run was sheer hell. The only thing keeping him alive was his willpower, and that seemed to be fading fast.

He managed, however, to keep his eyes forward, looking at the room only through the glasses. He hadn't been sure he'd be able to do that, but he found that Albert's bizarre experience was enough to sufficiently scare the hell out of him. He did not want that to happen to him.

The room went forward and then curved left in a

sharp U-turn. It was hard to navigate, hard to tell which way was forward and which way was back while weaving through the statues, especially when one was forced to concentrate hard on not looking at the dozens of stone figures that blocked the way at every turn.

Twice, the needle tip of an unseen spike gouged rudely into Wayne's skin, once in his arm and once in the soft meat of his right thigh. Another spike managed to scrape Brandy's hip as she walked past it, and she cursed loudly at it, but more in fear than in pain, Wayne thought.

Images of blood and death and terror bombarded him as he walked, trying to push past his mental defenses, reducing them much as a virus would whittle down his immune system. By the time he saw the next door, his body was trembling, his fists clamped together, white-knuckling the flashlight, his teeth clenched so hard he'd begun to feel sharp bolts of pain in his jaws. He had to draw on every ounce of his will just to keep moving.

Now he understood what Albert had been talking about. He couldn't imagine being in the sex room now. If the urges associated with that room were anything like what he felt now, then he could see how a person really could kill himself trying to satisfy such insane lust. Thank God he didn't give into temptation and sneak a peek at those statues.

He had almost reached the door when he felt a sharp, agonizing pain in his stomach.

Oh God! he thought as cold terror filled him. The images had become too much for him. He'd stopped being careful. When he saw the door, he stopped looking for the spikes, stopped watching for the real danger, wanting only to get away from those that were imaginary.

He looked down slowly, shielding his eyes from the horrors that loomed all around him, and lifted the glasses to examine his situation.

"Wayne?" Brandy asked, her voice trembling. "Something wrong?"

It was just an illusion. That was all. Like the one Albert suffered. He stared down at his stomach, looking at the tall, stone spike that came at him from the floor at such an angle as to spear him in the lower-right side of his belly.

It was just an illusion.

He could see the blood trickling down his waist.

"Wayne?" Brandy again, sounding more concerned.

It wasn't an illusion. This was real. Real blood. Real pain. Real trouble. He backed up slowly, pulling himself off the spike. He had not impaled himself very deeply, but he was a long ways from the nearest emergency room.

"What's wrong?" Nicole asked.

Wayne looked up at the door. This one appeared to be clear of the spikes that had circled the last one. Instead there were three more of these long, sharply angled spines protruding from the floor. "Nothing," he said. "There are some spikes coming out of the floor over here. Follow me close."

He embraced the pain and pushed on, using it to focus his attention.

The next room was yet another chamber. It was a smaller room, but was more densely populated with statues than any of the others. Wayne did not hesitate. He moved on, keenly alert for more deadly spikes.

Almost at once, he spied the next door, but statues blocked it. He would have to go around, get to it from the other side.

"I'm going to try and get us through this room," he explained. "Then we'll have to switch off again."

"That's fine," Albert told him. "Stop whenever you have to."

Wayne held his free hand firmly to his belly. He could feel warm, slick blood on his fingers. He hoped he could last that long.

The trip through this room took much longer than the rest. At an agonizingly slow pace, they worked their way between closely placed statues and past clusters of stone spikes. All four of them collected small cuts, scrapes and bruises along the way. Twice, they found themselves cornered and had to backtrack, and once they came back to the door from which they'd entered.

Horrible images surfaced in Wayne's mind every step of the way. Several times he stopped and squeezed his eyes closed, convincing himself that there was not something large and hairy stalking them on the ceiling or swarms of little, scurrying things spilling from the mouth of a screaming statue or gnarled, diseased hands reaching out for them from the darkness just beyond his vision. He could not understand why he was so convinced that these things were real. How could these statues possibly affect them like this? What kind of twisted mind could conceive of such a thing?

The four of them circled around and around until Wayne felt that he had finally reached his breaking point. And then, at last, the door was just ahead.

Wayne felt weak, drained, as though he'd spent the day doing hard labor instead of wandering this dark labyrinth. Feeling a little dizzy, thinking he must be well on his way to bleeding to death, he stood in the doorway leading out of the fear room's fifth chamber. He removed Brandy's glasses and peered into the next room. He peeked just a little at first, and then some more, and finally he braced himself and opened his eyes to the room ahead.

"Well, guys," Wayne said. "The good news is we're out of the fear room." He turned and gave Brandy back her glasses.

"And the bad news?" Asked Albert.

"See for yourselves."

Albert, Brandy and Nicole opened their eyes. The sixth chamber of the fear room was not a room of statues, but a room of stone spikes. There were thousands of them, standing up from the floor at random angles and heights, protruding from the walls and ceiling. Half a dozen columns stood in this room and these were each covered in long, deadly thorns. On the floor, covering almost every available square inch beyond the small area of smooth stone on which they stood, were literally thousands of tiny, needle-like spikes, each one pointing straight up.

"Watch your step," Wayne said. He turned and leaned against the wall beside the fear room door.

"Wayne, you're *bleeding*!" Nicole exclaimed.

"Yeah. I walked into one of those spikes."

"Oh my god!" cried Brandy. "Are you okay?"

Wayne shook his head. "I don't know."

Chapter 14

"Oh, that doesn't look bad," sighed Nicole. She was kneeling in front of Wayne, gently wiping away the blood with some gauze from Albert's first aid kit and examining the gash. "It's a pretty good cut," she admitted, "a little deep, but it's already stopped bleeding."

Wayne looked down at himself for the first time and realized that he was not really bleeding to death. He hadn't bled very much at all, in fact. It had run down his waist and to about the middle of his thigh, but that was all. "Then why do I feel so weak?" he asked.

"Do you ever get queasy at the sight of your own blood?" inquired Nicole.

Wayne shook his head. "Never."

Nicole thought for a moment. "Maybe it has something to do with those rooms, then."

He considered this. He *did* start to feel awful shaky in there. He was *still* trembling, in fact. "Yeah," he decided. "I think you're right. Mental exertion, I guess."

"You *were* leading for a long time," Albert agreed. "Longer than I did."

Wayne nodded and looked down at Nicole as she pressed a bandage over his wound. "How do *you* all feel?"

"*I'm* fine," Brandy replied.

"Yeah," Agreed Nicole as she stood up. "A little jittery, but that's all."

"Other than that weird attack I had," Albert added, "I'm perfectly fine."

Wayne nodded. "Then you don't think those spikes were poisoned, do you?"

Albert, Brandy and Nicole exchanged uneasy looks. Each of them had sustained some sort of cut, scrape or poke from at least one of those hateful things. If there was poison involved, then they had all been exposed.

"I took a pretty good poke early on," Albert said, looking down at the dried spot of blood on his arm. "I think if they were poisoned I'd probably be feeling it, too."

Wayne nodded. "Yeah. You're right. I just don't understand. It felt like I'd really hurt myself back there. I could've sworn I was bleeding to death."

"Maybe it was another illusion," Albert offered. "Like what happened to me, but based on a real injury instead of an imaginary attack."

Wayne nodded. "That could be right. I guess." He stood up straight, shaking it off. He felt embarrassed. He couldn't believe he'd created such drama over such a superficial injury. "I'll be fine. We should keep moving."

Albert hesitated. He wanted Wayne to regain his strength before moving on, but the four of them could not remain huddled here for much longer. They needed to keep moving. The blind man had made it clear that they needed to hurry. And he had no doubt that the longer they were down here, the more likely they were to attract a hound. Those creatures might already have grown bored with the underwear and begun to wander farther out into the temple. “Are you sure you can go on?”

“Yeah. I’ll be fine.” Wayne looked out at the tiny spikes on the floor, focusing his thoughts on the obstacles before them. He wanted to put this embarrassing injury behind him as quickly as possible. “Looks like there’s a path.”

There were small patches on the floor where there were no spikes, forming a sort of stepping stone path for them to follow.

“A safe path,” Albert agreed.

“Seems to defeat the purpose,” observed Wayne.

“Not really. This is the Temple of the Blind. The only way to get through those rooms back there was to be blind to the statues. But if you couldn’t see the rooms, you couldn’t see the path.”

That made sense. “You wouldn’t be able to find a way across if you couldn’t see,” Wayne reasoned. “So technically, a blind person couldn’t get through the Temple of the Blind. You have to be able to go back and forth, like we’re doing.”

“Exactly,” Albert agreed. “No one can accidentally stumble through it. You’d have to use something to blind yourself, like Brandy's glasses, or else feel your way around the rooms in the dark, which obviously isn't recommended with all these spikes."

"There weren't any spikes in the first room," Wayne recalled. "It probably would have been safe to just feel our way through there in the dark."

"I don't think I'd want to feel my way through *that* room," opined Nicole.

Brandy giggled. "You could probably still put an eye out in there," she agreed.

"I suppose you're right," remarked Wayne, grinning a little.

"I guess it's more like the Temple of the Nearsighted, huh," said Brandy.

Albert laughed. "Yeah. I guess it is." He stepped forward, examining the path ahead. "I think the rooms were designed to get harder each time. You can't ever get too confident that way. It's probably some kind of test."

"And we passed the test?" asked Nicole.

"Well, we're still alive," Albert replied. "I'd call that a pass."

"Tough grading curve," remarked Brandy.

"Let's go then," urged Wayne. He wasn't eager to see what the next test would be, but he certainly didn't want to stay here all night.

"I'll go first," Albert volunteered. "Everyone stay back a little bit." He walked up to the edge of the spiked floor and stepped onto the first "stepping stone" that led across the room. He then stepped carefully from one to the next, grimacing a little at the thought of what all those little needles would feel like if he missed and planted his bare foot on them. It would hurt like hell, no doubt, and probably send him stumbling back and into one of the many larger spikes.

"Be careful," Brandy pleaded. She could barely stand to watch.

"I am," he promised. With every step, he expected something more, some nasty little surprise, but there was nothing. Carefully, he made his way past the thorny columns to the doorway beyond.

The final step was a long one, requiring him to jump over the spikes, but it was hardly difficult. Once he was within the safety of the far door, he turned back and beckoned the others to follow.

One by one, the remaining three made their way cautiously across the spiked room to join him.

Chapter 15

The passage that led from the spike-filled room was just high enough for Wayne to walk through without being hunched forward and wide enough for Albert and Brandy to walk side by side and hand in hand. But the tunnel was sloped downward at such an angle that they were carried forward as they walked, forcing them to consciously slow down lest they risk slipping on the smooth stone floor.

"How are you feeling?" Albert asked, speaking to Wayne. "Any better?"

"Yeah, actually." His strength was coming back to him. "I guess it was the fear room after all."

"Mental exertion," Albert agreed. "And probably a

little bit of whatever those statues do to you."

Wayne nodded. "I guess so."

Nicole looked at Wayne, who was walking beside her. Their nudity had been forgotten by all but the slight chill in the air. The four of them could have been walking around in bathing suits. "You know," she said to him, "you haven't told us much about yourself."

Wayne shrugged. "I don't know much about you either," he retorted.

Nicole smiled. "Yeah. Fair enough. Let's see… I grew up here in Briar Hills—well, *up there* in Briar Hills—and so did Brandy. We're both juniors in college and we've been friends since we were kids. I'm a Special Education major and she's majoring in History. We're both twenty-one so when we get out of here you can take us both out for drinks." She flashed him a bright smile before continuing. "Albert's a sophomore and one of those Computer Science geeks. He's from St. Louis and he's *not* twenty-one so he has to stay home."

Albert turned and gave Brandy a comically hurt look that sent her into a fit of giggles.

"I'm not working right now but Brandy works at the

mall at Old Navy and Albert just recently started working at Staples. They met last year in chemistry class and got mixed up in all this stuff when someone sent them the box and its key. Now they live together."

Wayne nodded. "I see," he said, although he still wasn't entirely clear on the whole box story.

"So now you know stuff about us. Now it's your turn."

Wayne gave her an amused grunt. "Okay. Well, I'm originally from Springfield, but I've lived in Dunnen since I was about four. That's where I went to school. I'm a senior and I'm majoring in Art."

"Art?" Nicole interrupted, interested. "You didn't strike me as an artist."

Wayne shrugged. "I had three or four majors when I first came here. Finally, I just picked art. I like it. It works for me. I'm good at it."

Nicole nodded. "Do you work?"

"No. I'm a slacker. There's not much else to tell, really."

"Well," corrected Brandy, "except for you doing your roommate's girlfriend."

"Hey, I never actually *did* her. Besides, she hit on me, not the other way around. And I wouldn't have even considered doing it if I hadn't caught *my roommate* fooling around on *her*."

Nicole gaped at him. "No way!"

"Oh yeah. Some little blonde bimbo."

Brandy laughed. "I can see where the principles could get a little hazy there."

Wayne laughed. "That's what I'm saying!" He was feeling much better, actually. The stress of being in the fear room, of focusing so hard on seeing the spikes while not seeing the statues must have been a little too much for his brain. It was like trying to function without sleep.

He remembered clutching his belly as he walked and thinking that he must be slowly bleeding to death. Had that been something similar to what Albert experienced, when he thought something had attacked him and that he was dying? He supposed that if the statues could do that to Albert, then they certainly could make him believe that a superficial cut from one of those spikes was a mortal wound.

"So what kind of art do you do?" Nicole asked.

He shrugged. “Drawing. Painting. I had a sculpting class last year and really sucked at it. But I’ve been working a lot on computers lately. I’m not that great, but I’m okay. I guess.”

Nicole smiled at him. “That’s cool. I can’t draw shit.”

They fell into silence again as they walked, each of them wondering how long this tunnel would last. It seemed endless. They’d been walking for a long time and still there was no end in sight. The monotony of the gray stone was almost maddening.

“How close do you suppose we are to the end of this thing?” Wayne asked.

“No idea,” Albert replied. “Could be just ahead, could be we’ve barely started.”

“Knowing our luck,” Brandy said, “we probably aren’t anywhere near done.”

“Maybe this place just keeps on going forever,” Nicole added.

“I wouldn’t be surprised,” said Albert.

“How many clues do you have left in your box?” Wayne asked.

"Two."

Again, silence fell over them. The passage went on and on, until each of them had begun to wonder if it would ever end. How far down could they possibly go? How deep into the earth had they already traveled? It didn't seem possible that anything could go so deep.

But the passage did eventually end and the room that awaited them at the bottom was almost as big as the entrances to the emotion rooms.

They exited from one of several dozen doorways and walked out into the open chamber.

Brandy fished in Albert's backpack and removed the tube of sidewalk chalk. Albert had seen this at the store a few months ago and purchased it on a whim. It had seemed a much more useful tool for marking the way than the paint can. She used it to mark both sides of the passage they had just exited (Albert was amused to see that she wrote "Brandy + Albert" on one side in a big heart) and then returned the chalk to the tube.

In the very center, they found a single stone sentinel. It stood not straight and stiff like many of its kind, but in a casual pose, with its feet slightly apart and one arm dangling at its side. Its other hand was lifted, its long fingers curled into a sort of half-fist. Its head was cocked to one side. Even without a face, the sentinel seemed caught in a moment of pondering, confused by the many passages that surrounded it, as if wondering which way it should go.

Albert barely acknowledged the statue in the center of the room. He could see its meaning, and it was nothing he hadn't already guessed for himself. Only one way was the right way. The rest would take them to the maze or to some other horrible place they did not want to go. The real question was, which way was the right way?

The box would tell.

He did not have to retrieve it from the backpack. He knew what was inside. He'd looked the items over more times than he could count, daydreaming about this fantastic place, wondering what secrets may lie hidden beyond the fear room.

He began on the right and circled the room, shining his flashlight into each tunnel as he passed it. So far, the clues had been near the entrance to the tunnel he was supposed to take. This time would be no different.

On the far side of the room, in one of the last passageways that led off to the right, Albert spied something on the floor.

He stepped into the tunnel for a closer look and felt his stomach roll over as he realized what he was looking at. He stopped walking and actually took a step back.

"What is it?" Brandy asked from behind him.

Albert braced himself. This wasn't likely to be pleasant, but he had to go on. He walked up to the thing and knelt beside it for a closer look.

"Is that what I think it is?" Wayne asked, sounding sick.

Albert did not have to reply. Before him lay the mummified remains of a man. He leaned over it, examining it. There were no visible scars, no markings to indicate how he had died, not so much as a torn piece of clothing. After seeing the shattered bones in and around the decision room, he did not think that the hounds had been involved. But what did he really know about them? He still hadn't even seen one.

The man was lying in a pose that seemed unnatural, and Albert soon realized why. It looked to him as though the body had been dragged here from somewhere else in the temple. He could see where the shoulders of the man's jacket had been gripped while he was being moved.

The man was dressed to an earlier time, in a dark gray suit with a vest and tie, but he was well disheveled. The clothes themselves were covered with gray, clotted stains. From the left breast pocket of his vest hung a silver chain.

"It's Wendell Gilbert," Albert said, as fascinated by the body as he was repulsed by it. He stared at the corpse's white hair and shriveled face, still vaguely able to see the man from the newspaper clipping he now carried in his box. "This is where the pocket watch came from."

Wayne and the girls slowly approached him, looking almost as though they expected Wendell to sit up and say boo.

"So this is what happened to him," Brandy said thoughtfully.

Albert nodded. "Looks like he was after the same thing we are. Whatever that is."

"I'd say he didn't make it," said Wayne.

"He made it a long way," Albert pointed out. "Especially considering he's still wearing his clothes."

"Hey, yeah," Nicole said. "Why did he get to keep his clothes?" She crossed her arms over her breasts as she was again reminded that she was naked.

"Don't complain," Wayne said. "You're naked, but he's dead. I'd say you got the better end of the deal."

She was hardly able to dispute that reasoning.

Albert reached out and touched the corpse, patting at its chest and belly, repulsed by the hardness of the body. It was more like touching wood than flesh.

"What are you doing?" Brandy asked. She sounded disgusted and Albert could hardly blame her.

"I was hoping he'd have a journal on him, something we could use, but I guess not." He rose to his feet and looked down the tunnel ahead. "I guess we're going this way."

Wayne reached down and pulled a chunk of the gray stuff from one of Gilbert's sleeves. "It's mortar," he said, looking up at Albert.

"I know. I saw that."

“What does it mean?” asked Nicole.

“It means,” explained Albert, “that Wendell Gilbert came here right after he built those brick walls inside Gilbert House.” He looked down at the hands, the fingers half-curled in death. Even after all these decades, he could still see the gray residue that was caked on them. These were the very same hands that had smeared the mortar across the walls on the first floor of Gilbert House all those decades ago.

Brandy and Nicole stared at the body, unable to reply.

“He didn’t even bother to change,” Albert continued.

“What does that mean to us?” Nicole asked. “Is it important?”

Albert shook his head. “I don’t know. Probably not. It’s just curious. It certainly helps connect Gilbert House to the temple.” He turned and shined his light down the tunnel, wondering what lay ahead. “Come on. Let’s go.”

The four of them began to walk again.

“Bye, Wendell,” Wayne said humorlessly as he walked past the corpse. He did not feel too sorry for him. This was, after all, the maniac who built Gilbert House.

Perhaps the old man had only gotten what he deserved.

Chapter 16

The room at the end of this newest passage was empty, with a tall ceiling and a second door straight across from the first. It was almost identical to the one in which Beverly Bridger apparently went mad. The only difference was that this room was slightly larger.

Albert looked up at the ceiling, a feeling of deep uneasiness flowing into him, growing into something like dread. In what must have been his imagination, he faintly heard that far away sound of a chain as it rattled once and then fell silent.

"Something wrong?" asked Brandy. It seemed a stupid question to her. Of course something was wrong. She could see it in Albert's face. His expression always gave away his concern.

Albert shook his head. “It’s just…”

“Like the other one,” Nicole finished for him. “It’s like the one Beverly was afraid of.”

Albert nodded. “Yeah. Feels creepy here.”

Wayne looked up at the ceiling. There was only cold stone and emptiness. “I don’t feel any different than I did in the last room.”

Nicole agreed. She didn’t feel any difference either, but there was still something creepy about the room.

Brandy said nothing. Perhaps she did feel something, a creepy little tingle, an odd urge to brace herself for something scary, or maybe that was all in her imagination. After what happened to Beverly, she kept expecting some invisible talon to slash out of the darkness and tear out her heart.

“Let’s just keep moving,” Albert said. He did not like the empty rooms, especially after Beverly’s reaction to the first one. He had an odd feeling that if he possessed that psychic connection to a deeper, more intricate world that she apparently did, the room might not look so empty after all.

The four of them hurried through this room and into the next tunnel. Nothing attacked them as they crossed. Nothing tried to stop them. The room was empty. They were alone.

Ahead of them, a short distance down this next tunnel, Albert spied another abrupt drop and he forgot about the empty room. He peered into the lower passage with his flashlight. The floor of the lower tunnel was about six feet down, just like the ones they'd previously encountered.

He climbed down and searched the passage ahead with his light, his head cocked, listening.

Brandy sat down on the ledge behind him, meaning to follow him, but Albert motioned for her to stay back. "What is it?" she asked.

Albert hushed her. "Hounds," he explained after a moment.

"What?" Brandy sounded startled. "Do you see them?"

"No. Don't hear any, either, but they're here. Or at least they've been here before."

"How can you tell?"

"Scratches on the floor."

"The hounds made those?" Brandy asked.

Albert nodded. "I'm going to assume they did. The only other surfaces that were scratched up like this were in the room where we found that first one, the room with the dying sentinels. The blind man said they couldn't jump, so places like these must be like cattle guards to them."

"So what do we do?" Wayne asked.

"We be careful. Come on." He turned and gave Brandy and Nicole a hand. Then he stepped back and gave Wayne room to hop down.

"Hey," Wayne said, sounding concerned. "That weird blind guy said these things hunt by smell, right?"

"That's right," Albert confirmed. "That's why we had to go naked. I know it doesn't make any sense. If they can smell our clothes they can smell us."

"And I *know* they can smell blood." Wayne held out his hand, which was still smeared with dried blood from the cut on his belly.

Albert stared at Wayne's bloody hand for a moment. He was right. He had almost overlooked that detail.

"Let's just hope that they're all still keeping busy trying to get at our underwear."

"But last time you were down here," Nicole said, more than a little afraid, "One of them found its way back."

Albert nodded. "I know. If you hear that noise, head for higher ground. Remember, they can't jump."

"Says the creepy blind guy who stole our clothes," Wayne added.

He was right. They were trusting the word of a strange man who hadn't even allowed them a complete explanation. "It's all we've got," Albert replied.

The four of them continued on, each of them feeling jumpy, afraid that at any moment one of those horrible things would lunge out of the darkness, snapping and drooling.

"So you had a close encounter with one of these things?" asked Wayne.

"Damn near took my leg off," Albert recounted.

"So did you see what they look like?"

"No. We were too busy running for our lives."

Wayne nodded. That figured. He wished he had

some idea what it was they were up against. The unknown was always the most frightening.

The passage leading to the next room was longer than any of them would have liked. Albert wondered as he walked what the hounds were. Just the word "hound" made him think of hellish canines or raging wolves, but no dog that he could imagine would make the kinds of sounds they had heard while standing over that maze. So what the hell were they?

The tunnel suddenly opened up and the four of them stopped and gaped. They were standing on a stone bridge spanning what appeared to be an enormous chasm. It was only about thirty feet across, but they could see no walls for as far as their lights would reach both left and right, nor could they see a ceiling or a floor.

"Oh my god," said Nicole. She stared down into the darkness below them, amazed by the sheer size of this place. "It's like a canyon." On either side of them there was a sort of railing, a two and a half foot segment of wall, perhaps to keep the hounds from plunging to their doom.

To their left, just within sight, another bridge

spanned the seemingly bottomless gap, connecting two nearby tunnels. On their right and below them was another. A third loomed above them on the right, barely visible in the darkness.

The walls were not coarse rock, but the same smooth stone they had been seeing since they entered the temple. Whoever built the Temple of the Blind built this chasm along with it. But for what purpose?

Albert could also make out several open passages in the chasm wall without bridges, and he could too easily imagine rushing through the labyrinth, perhaps running from one of the hounds, and plunging into that bottomless darkness.

“It’s enormous,” Brandy marveled. “How big do you think this place is?”

Albert shook his head as he gazed down. He wished he’d thought to buy some flares. He could have dropped one of them over the edge to see how far down it fell. “Gilbert House was in another world. For all we know, we could be in that world now, or in some entirely other world. This labyrinth could be as big as a planet and we wouldn’t have a clue.”

Nicole stared down into the darkness below. She thought she could make out another bridge way down there somewhere, but she couldn't quite see that far. "How long do you think we could be down here?"

"There's no telling," Albert replied. "But the blind man seems to think we can do it, so it can't be too far. Besides, my box is almost used up. There's only one clue left."

"We should really keep moving," urged Wayne. He was looking back the way they'd come and thinking about the scratches on the floor.

Albert nodded. "You're right. Let's go." He started forward, thinking again about those flares. He could kick himself for not thinking of that. He could have dropped one off that other bridge, too, the one that stretched out over the maze. Maybe they could have caught a quick look at one of the hounds that way. Then he'd at least have some idea what they were up against.

Beyond the chasm, the passage led forward for another fifty yards before it abruptly ended in a wide chamber. Here, there were four new passages to choose from.

A sentinel stood guard at the center of this chamber. Like most of his kind, he offered no help. He was facing them as they entered, and stood with his feet together and his arms inquisitively outstretched, illustrating the choice with which they were faced.

The statue's feet and legs were covered in the same scratches that marred the floor around it.

As Albert walked to the first of these four tunnels, searching for the clue he knew had to be here somewhere, Nicole stopped and sat down on the cold, stone floor in front of the statue. "My feet are killing me," she groaned.

"Mine too," admitted Brandy. She leaned against the wall and rubbed her aching left foot.

Albert could feel the pain in his feet as well, but he dared not stop here to rest, not where there were scratches in the stone.

He found what he was looking for in the second tunnel. It was farther away than the other items had been, perhaps kicked out of place by one of the hounds, but it was there, the handle of an old, rusted dagger. He bent and picked it up, examining it. The blade had been shattered at its hilt, broken clean, but the piece in his backpack had been broken off at an angle. This indicated that there was at least one more piece of the blade, but he saw no sign of it in this passage.

But then again, there were also no bones in this passage. He'd seen no bones at all since the decision room, in fact. He remembered the way Wendell Gilbert's body had looked, how it had apparently been dragged to its final resting place from wherever he originally fell. He wondered how far people had actually made it through this labyrinth in the past. Surely no one could have gotten this far without the kind of clues he'd been given in the box. The blind man must have taken this dagger from another part of the labyrinth. The remaining piece or pieces were probably still where it was originally dropped.

"Something wrong?" asked Nicole.

"No. Just thinking."

"About what?"

"Just stuff. Nothing important. Come on. This is the way."

But before they could move, a noise rose in the darkness. It was a distant sound, but a violent one, a sudden roar that sounded more mechanical than organic. It was a hound.

"Come on," Albert urged. "*Hurry.*"

Nicole was off the floor and at Albert's side in a flash. Brandy and Wayne both hesitated a moment, their eyes wide, their ears sharp and alert, listening to the distant sound of apparent death, but then they, too, were moving.

The four of them rushed into the next passage. Behind them, the noise of the hound began to fade, the source apparently moving in the other direction, but they hurried anyway, terrified that it may still catch their scent and give chase.

In their fright, this tunnel seemed to go on forever, but soon enough the wall appeared ahead of them, the next passage elevated safely beyond the reach of the still-unseen hounds.

"God," Wayne said, panting. He turned and stared back as the others climbed into the higher passage. "I really don't like those things."

Albert nodded agreement. "It's such an odd noise they make. I can't place it."

“What do you think they are?” Brandy asked.

Albert had no idea. Nobody did. But the appearance of this one helped to support Albert’s theory about the scratches in the floor. There definitely seemed to be a connection between them. “Come on,” he said. “Let’s keep moving. My box is used up. We’ve got to be close now.”

Chapter 17

The passage abruptly tilted downward ahead of them, descending deeper into the darkness at a steep angle. “Careful,” warned Albert as he began to descend the hill. It would be easy to slip on such a steep surface, especially considering the smoothness of the stone on which they walked.

“Wouldn’t it have been easier to build steps?” Wayne wondered.

Albert gazed down at the floor, studying it with his flashlight. As usual, his mind immediately produced the worst possible explanation for such an irregularity: a ramp like this would allow access to an upper level for a creature unable to jump, just as a wheelchair ramp allowed access for people unable to climb steps. It was all too easy to imagine a hound charging up this hill toward them, making that horrible sound as it came. He reminded himself again that there were no scratch marks, but he knew that he had no actual proof that the hounds and the scratch marks were in any way connected. It was purely speculation. There could easily be another explanation for the scarred floors.

"I am so going to fall," said Brandy. "You just watch."

But she didn't fall. None of them did. Albert estimated their descent at about three stories before the passage finally leveled out and opened up.

The walls and ceiling sloped away, opening gradually into a large, high-ceilinged chamber. At the center of the room was an open space from which three more identical passages shrank away, creating a four-cornered star shape.

Albert stepped into the very center of the room and stopped. This didn't make any sense. Looking around him, there were four different passages. Discounting the one from which they had just entered, that left three entirely different choices, two of which were almost certainly wrong. But how were they supposed to know which way to go? The clues in the box had all been used up.

About twenty feet in front of him stood a single sentinel statue. Its back was turned to him and it was frozen in mid step as it walked away into the dark unknown beyond. Identical statues were on his left and right, each motionlessly walking away from him in their respective directions.

"Which way do we go?" asked Wayne.

"I have no idea. I'm out of clues."

"You've got nothing?"

Albert shook his head. He was staring at the sentinel in front of him. "The solution must be on one of the statues." Without waiting for a reply, he walked toward the one that was facing straight ahead. Aside from the fact that it was a sentinel, complete with featureless face and grossly elongated limbs, there was nothing unusual about it. It was in mid-stride, but relaxed, as though on a leisurely stroll. It had all its parts, and all its parts were as they should have been. Its hands were at its sides, frozen in mid-swing, its fingers splayed as naturally as fingers that long could possibly look. Its penis was limp (thankfully) and its muscles relaxed. Nothing about it indicated anything more than that it was walking.

He turned and shined his flashlight in the direction the sentinel was facing. He could not quite see to the tunnel that led away from the room.

Wayne, meanwhile, had approached the sentinel on the left and was examining the statue with his flashlight. "What am I looking for, exactly?"

"No idea," replied Albert.

Nicole and Brandy stood in the middle of the room, watching the two of them. The openness of the room made them nervous. The darkness seemed to push in at them from each of the four directions, threatening to swallow them.

Albert walked on past the statue. Soon, a second figure appeared, another sentinel, in exactly the same mid-stride pose as the others. "There's another statue up here," he reported.

Wayne turned and investigated the left passage. "Here too."

Nicole sat down on the cool floor and began to rub her aching feet. "You guys let me know if you figure it out."

Brandy followed her lead and sat down. Her feet were killing her. The stone floor had begun to punish her with every step.

Albert walked up to the farther sentinel and examined it. It was standing just a few feet from the next passage, seemingly on its way out of the room. He continued past the statue and into the tunnel ahead. It stretched forward a few yards and then opened up into a wide chamber that stretched well beyond the reach of his flashlight.

There was something there.

"Be careful," Brandy called.

"Don't worry." But with each step he grew more anxious. Wasn't this the part of the movie where the monster snatched up the idiot who strayed too far from the group?

The object that had drawn his attention was several yards inside the next chamber. For a moment he couldn't place it, but then he realized that it was another sentinel.

This one, however, was different than the others. It was much shorter, for one thing. At first he thought that the statue was kneeling, like the faith statue that stood before the flooded tunnel where they'd been forced to disrobe, but as he approached, he realized that this was not the case.

"Albert," Brandy called. "Come back. You're making me nervous."

"Just a minute." Albert examined this new chamber. The floor of the tunnel in which he was standing extended out into the new room only about six feet and then began to slope downward at a gentle angle. Just a few inches farther, the path ended. The rest of the floor was different. The smooth, gray stone gave way to a black and textured surface. A few yards beyond where the path vanished, the sentinel statue stood submerged to its waist in this new floor.

He walked to where the stone path ended and knelt, studying this darker surface. Reaching out, he touched it gently with his fingertips, lightly probing it, ready to snap his fingers back should something unexpected happen. The surface gave to his fingers, revealing a fine crust covering a thick black substance. He pulled his hand back and examined it. It was cold and wet, but also gritty, like mud. Curious, he lifted it to his nose and smelled it. It had an awful, rotten odor, like something dead.

He stood up and shined his flashlight at the wading sentinel. If the statue was complete and not truncated somewhere below its waist, then it would indicate the depth of this sludge to be approximately chest deep where it stood.

"Albert?" Brandy was beginning to sound impatient. He could hardly blame her. If she had wandered into a dark passage alone and lingered he'd be impatient too.

"Coming." He backed away from the mud, still staring at it. Could this be the way they were supposed to go? He stared past the statue, into the darkness beyond. He dared not imagine what kinds of horrors might wait in this chamber if it was not the correct path.

He turned and hurried back to where Brandy and Nicole still sat, pausing only to wipe the mud from his fingers onto the smooth stone wall of the tunnel.

"Find anything?" asked Brandy.

"Maybe."

Before he could describe what he'd found, Wayne reported his find from the other passage. "Hey guys, this room's flooded."

"Oh great," spat Nicole.

Albert turned, interested. "With mud?"

"What? No. Water."

"Just water?"

Brandy and Nicole gazed up at Albert, curious.

"Yeah. Just like we swam through after we took our clothes off."

Albert stared down the empty tunnel at Wayne's light, thinking.

"What's up?" Wayne asked.

"This one over here's filled with some kind of black mud."

"What?" Wayne started walking toward him now.

"Mud?" asked Nicole.

Albert nodded. "Mud. Looks like it's pretty deep." He turned and shined his light toward the third passage. There was mud in one room, water in the second, so what was in the third? "I'll be right back."

He walked down the third passage, pausing briefly to

examine both of the statues along the way. These were identical to those he'd just seen, as was the layout of the tunnel and the room beyond, but it was immediately obvious that what filled this room was neither water nor mud. This was something else entirely.

"What do you see?" Wayne asked from behind him.

"I'm not sure." Albert knelt at the edge of the path and examined the fluid. It was not black like the mud, but a sickly sort of yellowish brown. It was translucent, allowing him to see just a few inches beneath its surface.

"What is it?" Wayne asked.

Albert didn't know. He reached down and cautiously dipped his fingers into it, half expecting to be burned by the mysterious fluid, but it was as cold as the mud. When he pulled his hand back, the brownish fluid oozed off his hand like cold motor oil.

"Looks like snot or something," Wayne observed.

"Let's hope not." Albert lifted his finger carefully to his nose and smelled it as he had done the mud. There was no stench of rot, only a subtle odor of something dank and perhaps moldy, like an old, wet cellar.

"Any idea what it is?"

"None whatsoever." He stood up and looked around. The room itself was identical to the last. The same half-submerged sentinel stood a short distance beyond the reach of the path, still trudging toward its mysterious destination. The only difference was what they would have to wade through. "Come on."

The two of them turned and walked back to where the girls were sitting.

"So what did you find?" asked Nicole.

"We're not sure," Albert replied. "Some kind of oily stuff. I have no idea what it is."

Brandy wrinkled her nose. "'Oily stuff?'"

"Kind of reminds me of clean motor oil," Albert described.

"Lovely," Nicole sighed. "Tell me that's not the way we have to go."

"I really don't know yet." Albert walked over to the sentinel that faced the water and began to study it. "We're out of clues so one of these guys has to tell us the way."

"Didn't look to me like they were talking," said Wayne. He sat down near the girls and sighed, relieved to be off his feet.

Albert's feet ached too, but he couldn't stop. He went from one statue to the next, beginning with those on the left, then moving to the passage that led to the mud and finally back to the third passage, but none of them gave anything away. They were perfectly identical.

"I don't get it," he said at last as he returned to where the others were sitting. He stood staring into the darkness, thinking.

"Maybe it doesn't matter which way we go," Wayne suggested.

"I doubt it. We're supposed to stay on the path."

"So how do we know which one to take?" Wayne pressed.

Albert didn't know.

"Did we take a wrong turn?" asked Brandy.

"We couldn't have," replied Albert. "We followed all the clues, just like the blind man said."

"Maybe we made a mistake," suggested Wayne, and Albert suddenly felt very nervous. He remembered again the way Wendell Gilbert's body had been moved. He also remembered the missing pieces of the dagger. Was it possible that someone had rearranged the clues?

But how? Who else could be down here?

No. That couldn't be right. The blind man had told them to trust the box. Surely he would have been aware of someone tampering with the clues. He seemed, after all, to know exactly where and when to find them in this enormous labyrinth. What other choice was there?

Wayne swung his flashlight from one passage to the next. "All the statues are walking off in different directions," he saw. "Maybe it means we're supposed to split up."

"No," Brandy said, her eyes suddenly wide. "Uh-uh. I'm not going anywhere alone."

"Me either," agreed Nicole.

Albert considered the idea for a moment. It was a sound guess, and it was obvious that the three visible sentinels were going their own separate ways, but splitting up just didn't seem right. "I don't think so. For starters, there are only three passages and four of us."

"What makes you think anybody knew how many of us would come down here?" Wayne asked. "I don't think I buy that whoever built this place could see into the future."

"True," Albert agreed. Although it wasn't an idea he would entirely dismiss, not after all that he'd seen. "But then what would be the point of splitting up? What if there was only one of us?"

Wayne shrugged. He never claimed to have all the answers.

"And we couldn't just leave somebody behind down here."

Nicole gave a visible shudder as she tried to imagine sitting there on the cold floor, watching three flashlights disappearing in three different directions, leaving her all alone.

"Well that's all I've got," Wayne said. "What's your idea then?"

Albert looked back at him without speaking. He didn't have an idea. He was fresh out. The statues weren't talking and his box had finally failed him. He literally had no clue what they were supposed to do now. For all he knew, perhaps Wayne was right. Perhaps they were simply supposed to go their separate ways. But he really didn't think so. The dying sentinels in the decision room had also each been reaching toward a different passage, but only one of those had been the correct path.

Nicole shifted her weight and leaned back, stretching her legs out in front of her and gazing up at him. "You'll figure it out," she assured him. "You've done it every other time."

But Albert wasn't sure if he was going to be able to keep coming up with the answers. Until now he'd begun to feel like a magician, finding another fascinating trick every time he reached up his sleeve or into his hat, but in the end he simply didn't know all the magic tricks, and he was afraid he might finally be running out of illusions.

He turned and stared into the darkness that led to the mud. No matter which way they went, they were going to have to enter something unpleasant. The water would be the ideal path. Water would only make them wet and cold, and perhaps there was something in it that masked their scents, explaining the blind man's insistence that they relinquish their clothing. The mud and the oil were different. They certainly would not be getting out clean, and who knew what was really in those chambers. The stench of the mud might attract the hounds. Or perhaps something lived in it, something even more terrifying than the hounds. And who knew what that oil was.

"And you think it would be dangerous to just pick one," Wayne said.

"Very dangerous," Albert confirmed. He thought about the oily substance. What in the world was that stuff, exactly? Was it flammable? Was it corrosive? It hadn't burned his fingers but that didn't mean it wouldn't if exposed to it long enough. It looked almost like bile. He felt a hard shiver as he suddenly thought about the carnivorous pitcher plant, which attracted insects into hooded jugs and trapped them in a pool of digestive enzymes. What if they waded out into that stuff, too far out to return, and their flesh began to melt away? It would be a horrible way to die.

"Then what do we do?" asked Brandy.

Albert sat down on the floor in front of Nicole and tried to think. There were no more clues. The statues gave nothing away. It didn't make sense, really. Why would the blind man give them all the clues to get this far and then leave them stranded here? There was simply no logic in that.

Nicole sat up straight and began rubbing her feet again. Albert understood how she felt. His feet were also aching. He looked over at Brandy. She was sitting with her eyes closed, resting while she had the chance. The next tunnel could lead them back into hound-infested territory and she might not have this chance again. It was good for them all to rest.

Albert closed his eyes for a moment, too, relaxing. Rather than focusing on the horrors of the wrong path, he tried to focus on the fact that one of these passages had to be the correct one. That meant that one of them was safe. As much as he hated the thought of getting cold and wet again, the water was the most appealing choice. But it also seemed the least likely, simply *because* it was the most appealing. Although that wasn't the kind of logic he was willing to bet his life on. Of the other two, he thought the oil would be the better choice. If he knew the path was safe, he could simply grit his teeth and ignore the funky feel of it against his naked flesh. It would be gross, but it would not be quite as bad as the rotten-smelling muck that waited in the middle passage.

He shrugged out of his backpack and removed the

box from within. As he opened it and peered in at the contents, something stirred in the back of his mind.

Wayne watched him as he opened the box. This was only the second time he'd seen it. The first was when he stuffed Beverly's envelope inside it to keep it from getting wet while they swam the flooded tunnel.

Albert removed the tightly-folded envelope with Beverly's file in it and then stared for a moment at the things inside the box. He reached in and stirred through them, as though rearranging them might make the hidden meaning of this puzzle clearer. Two pieces of a stone finger, broken from the warning statue in the very first room. An old button from a heavy blue fabric, draped over the outstretched arm of a dying sentinel. The feather and the bird scratched into the sentinel's neck. Wendell Gilbert's pocket watch, gruesome but vividly clear. Finally, the broken blade. It should have been the last clue. The only other things in the box were the small, leather pouches which contained the key to the box and the gold coins. There should have been no more decisions left to make. What could he be missing?

He reached in and picked up the sentinel's fingertip,

the piece of the statue that he had found in the first passage the year before. That had been such an easy clue, once he'd figured out what he was looking for. Why couldn't this be as easy?

He picked up the other piece of the finger, the one that had been given to him in the box, and pieced them back together.

"Mind if I look at that?" Wayne asked.

Albert dropped both pieces of the finger back into the box and slid it over to him. Maybe a fresh mind would be able to bend around whatever it was he was missing. He picked up Beverly's folded envelope and brushed away the grime it had collected from the dirty clues inside the box.

He looked back at Nicole, who was staring down at her feet as she rubbed them. She was tired. He could tell. She sat with her knees slightly bent, her bare feet resting on their heels, slightly apart. He could see the dark hair between her thighs, the soft fold across her navel as she sat slouched, and the round curves of her firm breasts. He turned and looked at Brandy again, his girlfriend, the love of his life. She had opened her eyes again, but now she was staring up at the ceiling. Her knees were together. He could not see that pretty place between her legs, but he could see her pert breasts and he again felt jealous that the sight was not his alone.

He wondered what she was thinking. Perhaps she was remembering Olivia and Beverly. Or perhaps she was thinking about the blind man and the sentinels. Or perhaps she was thinking nothing at all but that she was tired and ready to go home.

Maybe they should just turn back. Was it really worth it? It was a thought that had crossed his mind more than once since watching the pool of blood slowly spread across the floor beneath Beverly's motionless body. He could still vividly remember that tragic scene, and it was far too easy to picture Brandy in her place.

He looked back at Nicole, not wanting to think about such terrible things. She had stopped rubbing her feet and was now just staring at them. She looked so tired. What the hell was he doing to them? He lowered his eyes, not wanting to see that weariness on her face, and found himself looking at her feet. She had pretty feet. She had slender, well-groomed toes and her skin was soft and smooth. The soles of her feet looked soft, almost pink in the light, and something tickled way back in his brain again.

He looked at Wayne, still feeling that odd little tickle. He was staring down into the box, trying to think. Unlike the girls, he didn't appear weary, merely frustrated as he tried to locate a solution to their situation from the puzzling array of objects before him. In the glow of the flashlights, his body was very pale, almost white, except for those places on him that were dark: his hair, his eyes, the dried blood on his belly.

Something was wrong. He stared at Wayne, trying to grasp what it was that he was missing. It seemed to be barreling toward him like a freight train, but still he couldn't grasp it, couldn't understand it. He looked at Brandy. What the hell was it?

"What are we going to do?" Brandy asked. She was still staring up at the ceiling, her skin soft and milky in the pale light.

Another tickle.

Albert closed his eyes for a moment, squeezing them tightly as if to shake away a bad image, and then opened them and peered over at the sentinel that faced the water. It was obvious that they were supposed to go in one of those three directions, but how were they supposed to know which one? They needed a clue, and yet all of his clues had been used up.

He considered the coins. The man with no eyes had gifted them to him at the end of their first adventure down here. They did not seem like a clue at the time, and he could think of nothing now that might connect them to any of these chambers. Yet they were the only items left in the box, which that same, eyeless man specifically told them to use before scurrying away with their clothes.

When he looked back at Nicole and Brandy, they were both looking at him, waiting for him to reveal the answer, as he always did. Looking back at them, he felt that tickle grow a little.

They had four choices. They could go forward, wade through mud, perhaps get swallowed in the muck, never knowing if they were going the right way. They could go left, swim through freezing water, never knowing if there was another end to be reached, perhaps drown in those cold, still depths. Or they could go right, into whatever that other stuff was, swimming for all they knew in a pool of pure poison. The only other way was back the way they'd come. A long, hard journey back home was all that awaited them there, with no answers, no closure. It was only home. And the phone would probably be ringing.

He looked again at Nicole. She was beautiful. Her complexion was slightly darker than Brandy's, because she had spent more of her summer tanning, but her skin was still a soft and lustrous color in the dimness around her. He looked at her feet again, at the soft, clean skin of her soles and toes, and that tickle grew into a tingle and then a roar.

He looked down at his hands. They were pale and soft in the light, except for his fingers, which were dirty from handling the items inside the box and brushing the dirt from Beverly's envelope. He looked down at the rest of his naked body, then at Wayne and Nicole and then at Brandy, who had sat up to watch his odd behavior. It had been there the whole time and he hadn't seen it for its subtleness.

"What is it?" Nicole asked. She could tell that he knew something. She could see it in his eyes. Something was stirring up there. He'd found some more pieces to this puzzle and they were all flying together in his mind.

Albert reached over and took the box back from Wayne. He withdrew the pocket watch and ran his fingers across its tarnished lid. There was a thin, gritty film on it that clung to his clean fingertips. He reached inside the box and ran his fingers all the way around its smooth interior. They came away nearly black with grime. He remembered when he first opened the box in the second floor lounge with Brandy, thirteen months ago. He remembered noticing how dirty the contents of the box had been, as though someone had gathered the objects off the dirty ground…

"There was another clue…" he said, almost in awe.

"What?" Brandy was staring at him, confused.

Albert held his hand up for her, showed her the dirt on his fingers. "Look. The box was dirty."

All three of them stared at him, waiting for him to continue.

He put the box down and rose to his knees in front of Nicole. He grabbed her foot and lifted it, making her cry out in amused surprise. "Look at your feet. Look at your hands, your knees, your butts. You've all walked, sat and crawled on your bellies through this place!"

Brandy looked down at herself, remembering the tight squeeze through the tunnel just past the maze. "We're clean," she said.

"Exactly!" He kissed Nicole's foot, as much for emphasis as in excitement and she jerked it away with a giggle. It had tickled.

"But the clues were all filthy, like someone threw dirt in with them."

"Or mud…" said Wayne, finally understanding. He turned and looked back into the passage behind him. "Mud from *that* passage."

Albert remembered the way he'd shaken the box when he first received it, wondering what was in it, probably reducing a clump of dried mud to a fine dusting of dirt. Then, when he and Brandy opened it and examined the contents, he had simply wiped away the dust and dirt without even thinking, assuming that the items had simply been filthy when they were gathered together and locked inside.

But why would items taken from a place as clean as

this be dirty?

Wayne turned back and looked at Albert. "And you're a computer science major? Did you ever consider forensics?"

"Yeah. But I found it too disturbing,"

Wayne smiled. "Yeah. Disturbing." He remembered the fear room and the pit of spikes and would have laughed if not for the seriousness of those things.

"So how do we know it's the mud and not the oil, or whatever that other stuff is?" Nicole asked.

"I don't know what that stuff is," Albert replied, "but I think we could tell it apart. I'm not sure that stuff would ever dry into dirt." He remembered the hard crust he had poked his fingers through when he first examined the mud. A small chunk of that stuff would have fit nicely into the box.

"So we have to go down *there*?" Nicole asked, not sounding particularly pleased by the discovery.

"Come on." Albert stuffed the envelope back into the box, then the box back into his backpack. He was already walking toward the next tunnel as he slipped it back over his shoulders.

Chapter 18

The flashlights could not reach across the mud. There was no way to know if this room contained a pool, a lake or a sea. Albert stared down at the black surface, wondering. The rest of the temple had been solid stone except for the one pool of water. Elsewhere, there had not even been a thin layer of dust to dirty their feet. Where would something like this come from? Was it actually carried in here, perhaps bucket by bucket? Or was there some sort of inlet? And for what? Just to make them suffer through it to get to the end of this strange journey? It was like something out of a bad movie.

"This isn't going to be pleasant, is it?" asked Wayne.

"Probably not," Albert replied bluntly. He had no

idea what could be in sludge like this. He didn't even want to know. He stepped forward, planting his bare foot into the mud. The surface had dried into a thin, brittle crust, but beneath it, the mud was cold and wet. It squished beneath him and oozed up over his foot and between his toes.

"I don't know if I can," Brandy said. "This is way worse than the water."

"We don't know what could be in there," Nicole agreed.

Albert could hear the dread in their voices, and when he turned, he could see it clearly on their faces, too. "We don't have a choice," he reminded them. "This is the right way. We can't turn back now."

But Brandy wasn't convinced. She stared out at the black and putrid path before them, her eyes filled with fear.

"Just take my hand," he urged. "I'll be right beside you."

Reluctantly, Brandy took his hand and followed his lead. She said nothing, but grimaced terribly as her foot and ankle sank beneath the surface.

"All the clues led us here," Albert said, trying to convince himself as much as anyone else. "That means this path is safe. There's no telling what might have happened if we'd gone into one of those other rooms."

"It's absurd, if you ask me," Wayne said as he watched Albert and Brandy step out into the mysterious muck. With each step, their feet came up black. "First, we have to get naked and now we have to swim through mud? What's next? A wrestling arena? I'm seriously starting to think somebody's filming this."

Nicole stepped in next and let out a long, soft squeak of disgust. "It's awful!" she squealed as she waded deeper and deeper into the frigid sludge behind her friends. It quickly crept up her legs to her knees and she reached out and grabbed Albert's elbow as much for physical support as mental. It sucked at her feet, resisting her with each step.

Wayne followed behind them, barely able to hold back a cry of disgust as his foot sank and a foul smell rose up around him. He watched those in front of him, the way they pushed on together, clinging to one another, and was reminded that he was, after all, just a stranger to them. He wished he had someone to cling to him that way, giving him strength, but it had been a long time since he'd had anyone like that. So he stayed back, pushing on alone.

"Not so bad," Albert urged through chattering teeth, trying to keep his companions' spirits up, but it was pointless. For one thing it *was* that bad. The mud was thick, especially near the bottom, and as it rose up their thighs, it became clear that it would not be an easy trip. And the stench was unbelievable. It reeked like rotting garbage. Could this be some kind of giant compost heap?

"Oh god this is gross," Nicole groaned. It was easily as cold as the water they swam through earlier that night, perhaps colder. It numbed her skin and sent a shiver deep into her body.

Brandy said nothing. She looked to Albert as though she were barely biting back a scream.

"Why would someone make something like this?" Wayne asked.

"There's got to be a reason for it," Albert assumed. "Maybe it's some kind of test. Maybe it's just to see how much we want it."

"You'd think they'd have been satisfied after their fucking fear room," Wayne grumbled.

"You'd think," Albert agreed.

As it became stirred up beneath them, so was its odor, and soon a dank, moldy stench of decay surrounded them. And as the filthy stuff squished against the sensitive flesh of their exposed genitals, not one of them could repress the groans and whimpers that rose from their throats. The awfulness of that cold, reeking sludge oozing into the folds of their soft skin was almost more than any of them could stand.

"Maybe it masks our scent from the hounds," Albert suggested, trying hard to find a positive thought.

"That would make more sense than just water," Wayne agreed.

It grew steadily deeper as they went, sliding up over their hips and waists to their bellies. And as it grew deeper, it grew more challenging. Soon they were struggling for every step. It seized their legs and sucked at their backs, like a living thing, attempting to impede their progress. Furthermore, it churned around them, belching and squelching against their naked flesh, spewing that putrid stench with every step they managed.

It was now that Albert had an awful thought. What if that stench was not of rotting garbage but rotting corpses? What if this room was some sort of hellish graveyard? He could almost picture his foot sinking through the mud and into the putrid skull of some rotten carcass, squashing black jelly that used to be a brain between his bare toes. It was a thought that almost made him gag, but one he would have to keep to himself. It would do no good to speak such horrors aloud, as it would have done no good to speak any of the horrors that had crossed his mind today.

He wondered if it was healthy to keep so many terrible thoughts bottled up inside, and immediately remembered the corpses he'd found in Gilbert House. Nick and Trish. Was it normal, he wondered, to walk away from such a thing without being sick? He thought of Beverly Bridger's body, sprawled on those horrible spikes, and how he had turned away from her and just kept going. He had simply buried those disturbing things within himself and moved on. He wondered if that said anything about the state of his mental health.

Soon, they were up to their chests in the black muck and the half-submerged sentinel was swallowed in the darkness at their backs. Nicole's breasts seemed almost to float upon the surface as she struggled forward, barely keeping her balance. She was holding Albert's arm up high, not wanting to dirty her hands.

Brandy, however, had already tumbled forward a couple of times and was covered to her neck in stinking sludge. Her flashlight had gone under with her each time and now the light shined out in a broken beam through a filthy lens.

Albert had feared that this obstacle would prove impossible, that it would get deeper and deeper until it swallowed them, that they would drown with their mouths and lungs filled with reeking sludge, but as they pushed on, the mud grew no deeper. It seemed that the sentinel had shown them the deepest part. Furthermore, the mud remained thin enough to allow them to move through it, although not without considerable effort. It remained dense only at the bottom, where it continued to suck at their feet, resisting each step they took.

Nicole's feet caught in the mud and she fell forward

with a yelp, barely keeping her face above the surface. Her flashlight vanished into the muck and with it went her share of the light. When she had gotten her feet back under her, she was a mask of darkness from her chin down. Her hair, the backs of her shoulders and her face were the only parts of her that remained clean.

Albert glanced at her and then at Brandy. "Well, at least we're not exactly naked anymore."

Nicole made a sick noise in her throat. "I think I'd prefer to just let you and Wayne stare at my tits, actually."

"I don't think I was *staring*, was I?" Albert asked.

Brandy gave him a sharp jab with her elbow and he was amused by the dirty look she shot him. At least she wasn't so overwhelmed by the mud that she couldn't still put him in his place.

"*I* might have been staring once or twice," Wayne said. "Sorry."

Nicole grinned a little in spite of her disgust.

They'd gone just a few steps farther when Brandy lost her balance and vanished all the way to her bangs in the sludge. She scrambled to stand up, spitting and clawing at the revolting mess that clung to her face and spewing an obscene barrage of curses.

For a moment, her glasses were gone, swallowed by the mud, but she located them quickly and was still trying to wipe the mud away with her filthy hands when the light at their backs vanished and they heard Wayne gagging and spitting.

A little farther along, Nicole stumbled again, this time taking Albert with her. It oozed into his mouth and the taste was indescribably awful, bitter and grimy, more like metal than dirt, but with the grotesque sweetness of something long rotten. He pulled his face from the mud and spat viciously, gagging violently as his brain again tried to bring up the image of a soupy corpse lying beneath his feet.

If not for the nauseating stench and the biting cold, these events might have been comical, like the antics of a children's comedy. But not one of them felt like laughing. If the other side did not come into view soon, sheer exhaustion would drag them down with Albert's imaginary corpses, and the only idea that Albert found more repulsive than walking on them was becoming one of them.

But they would not end up that way. At last, as their legs and backs began to ache from the exertion of pushing through the thick muck, it began to recede. It slid back down their chests and bellies and thighs, but left a thick skin upon their bodies so that they resembled black, lumbering beasts trudging through the darkness.

They could no longer see the walls on either side of them. The room had widened into an immense cavern. Ahead of them and slightly to the right, a doorway appeared in a great wall of smooth, clean stone. A large, stone archway surrounded the door, intricately carved with images they could not yet make out.

The four of them stepped out of the mud, wiping at the stinking mess with their filthy hands, unable to clear it all away but trying nonetheless.

"Any chance there's a shower down here?" Nicole asked through chattering teeth. She wiped the majority of the mud from her arms, grimacing at the nauseating stench that now wafted from her entire body. She shook the mud from her slender fingers, splattering the clean wall and floor with globs of wet, black goo, and then turned and spat onto the floor.

Brandy groaned. "I'll never feel clean again." She raked the goop from her chest and belly and flung it to the floor. Then, in an uncharacteristically unladylike display, she bent and clawed the disgusting muck from between her legs. She hated the feel of it on her bare skin. She wanted it off of her and she wasn't concerned with being dainty about it.

Albert wiped absently at his arms as he approached the archway and examined it. The carvings were of people, thousands of people, piled together as if in a sea of human flesh. He could see heads and legs and arms, feet and hands, breasts, bellies, buttocks and backs. They were not simply a pile of body parts, like the result of some mass slaughtering, but the bodies of living people, all entwined together. Some appeared to be in the throes of orgasmic bliss, others in the midst of a furious rage. Some were lost in their own misery and others seemed terrified beyond their own imaginations. Some of the faces were even familiar. Albert recognized them as statues from the sex room. Perhaps these were all the statues from all of the rooms, all of them intricately carved here in this eternal sea of human beings. There even seemed to be emotions depicted that they had not faced in any of the emotion rooms. Avarice. Sorrow. Jealousy. Joy.

"Wow," Nicole said, gazing at the carvings. It seemed to instill a little of each of the emotions it depicted, probably because it did contain faces from the different rooms, but the overall feeling was not like the chaotic tangle that met the eyes. It was something else, something much more peaceful, a medley of feelings that summarized the entire human heart.

Albert nodded. Wow indeed. "I think this is it," he said, staring through the archway at the wide corridor beyond. He turned his head and looked at Nicole. She was smeared with mud from her face to her feet, her hair matted with it.

Brandy stepped up beside her, also gazing at the carvings. Her light blonde hair was now black from the crown of her head down.

Looking at the two of them, Albert thought that there was something erotic about the sight, even though the stuff that clung to their skin was vile and rank. Their flesh was now partially hidden, their bodies concealed from his view except for the pale, pink streaks where they had wiped it away with their hands. He could still see their shapes and he had an urge to turn and wipe it away from Brandy's body, if only for the excuse to touch her gorgeous skin.

"Come on," Albert urged, forcing his thoughts back to the task at hand. It wasn't hard. The cold and the stench and the simple awfulness of the mud were more than adequate for keeping him focused.

The four of them passed through the archway and started forward. The tunnel beyond was different from the others. It was made of the same gray stone, was filled with the same cold darkness, yet it seemed warmer somehow, more inviting. About twenty yards into the tunnel, wide steps descended down a short distance. It was at the foot of these that he paused and listened. "Do you hear that?"

"Hear what?" Brandy asked.

Albert shook his head. "I don't know." It was too faint to hear clearly, and now it seemed to be gone. He moved on, not wanting to waste any time.

The tunnel continued this way, traveling straight for about twenty yards to a set of steps that led down perhaps half a story and then repeating. As they approached the third set of steps, Albert paused again and listened. This time he knew he heard something. "Do you hear it now?"

Brandy, Nicole and Wayne exchanged a curious look. They heard nothing at all. Not a sound.

"It's very soft…I think it's…" He shook his head. He couldn't place it, but he *could* hear it. He started moving again and the others followed. Shortly after descending the next staircase, Brandy paused and listened. "Do you hear it?" he asked.

Brandy shook her head. "I thought I did…but I guess not."

Albert looked up into the darkness ahead, a little confused. Surely he wasn't imagining it.

They went on.

Nicole turned as they walked and looked back the way they'd come. "I hope no one gets mad at us for not wiping our feet," she said, almost absently.

Albert grinned. "If it bothers them, they should've put a mat in front of their mud hole."

Brandy stopped. Now she *did* hear something. "Singing," she said.

"What?" Nicole was looking at her as if she'd lost her mind.

"I hear singing," she explained. She was staring up into the tunnel.

Albert nodded. That was exactly what he heard. Singing.

"Maybe I've got mud in my ears," Nicole guessed. She could hear nothing.

They walked a little farther through the tunnel, toward this mysterious singing, and soon another archway appeared in front of them, seemingly identical to the last. Something else was there too, hunched in the darkness beyond it, waiting for them. It stood up as they approached, and they saw at once that it was the blind man who'd taken their clothes.

"You succeeded!" he said, sounding not just pleased but ecstatic. He moved toward them a few steps, and they saw that he was limping a little, nearly staggering. "Come!"

As they approached the archway, which was indeed

identical to the last, they became aware of a vast space looming ahead of them, larger than any chamber they'd witnessed so far.

"Come! Come!" the blind man called to them as they approached, motioning them into the darkness behind him.

They stepped past him, through the archway, and marveled at what they saw.

"Welcome!"

Albert stared, astonished. It surpassed his wildest imaginations. It was more than he'd ever dreamed possible.

"What is it?" Brandy asked.

Albert had no way of knowing, no way of even dreaming, but he had named the Temple of the Blind, and so he named this place as well. "City of the Blind," he replied. "It's a City of the Blind."

Chapter 19

There had been several chambers that were impossible to see across with merely their flashlights, but beyond the final archway was a chamber that was far more immense than any before it. The very feel of the air was different here, as if they had just stepped out beneath an open night sky.

Directly ahead of them, two stone towers rose up into the darkness. They were each at least sixty feet across, perfectly cylindrical, with hundreds of small, square holes that looked to Albert like windows in a skyscraper. These same square holes were cut into the wall behind them as far as they could see, all of them perfectly spaced in a vast grid.

"Unbelievable," sighed Brandy as she gazed up into the open darkness. Albert had called this place a city of the blind, and she had no doubt that he was right. But it wasn't a city that came to mind when she stared at those huge towers. "It looks like…a *hive*."

Nicole cocked her head and listened. Now she heard something, a faint sound that might have been the singing Brandy mentioned.

Wayne heard it too, very soft, very distant. He could not tell which direction it was coming from.

The blind man limped past them and began hobbling into the darkness that waited ahead of them. He moved with brilliant excitement, almost ecstasy, but also with obvious pain, like an old man whose best years were far behind him. It was almost sad to watch. Could this really be the same man who leapt to the ceiling with their clothes and scurried away like a blind and naked Spiderman? "Hurry!" he told them, and they followed, curious to see where he would lead them.

As they approached the two stone towers, three more came into view deeper into the city.

"It's enormous," Albert marveled. "It just keeps

going."

Something else appeared out of the darkness then. It was not another tower, but rather the opposite. The blind man had been veering toward one of the two towers, rather than passing directly between them, and Albert now saw why. There was a hole in the ground, its diameter as wide as the towers that surrounded it. It plunged into an unimaginable darkness far below, and as they walked around it, Albert saw that the same square openings lined the walls as far down as he could see. It looked exactly like the towering columns that surrounded it, but inverted.

He looked up into the vast darkness overhead, wondering. The ceiling was not visible, but he felt certain that if he could see it, he'd find more of those holes above them. Brandy had been right. It *was* like a hive, complex and multi-chambered.

"Where are we going?" Wayne asked.

The blind man did not answer. Instead, he raised one hand and pointed into the darkness ahead.

For several minutes they walked, their pace quick, almost jogging to keep up with the ecstatic old man who navigated the darkness without eyes. But as they passed close by one of the stone towers, Albert paused long enough to gaze into one of the square openings, probing it with his flashlight. At first, they had looked like windows, but why would a place like this, a place so utterly removed from the light, have windows? Peering inside, he found a very small and empty room. The opening was the only way in or out. Were these sleeping chambers? Were these tiny spaces all homes for the inhabitants of this city? And if so, where were all of these inhabitants? Nothing stirred for as far as he could see. No faces peered out at them. The city, in all its massiveness, seemed to be as dead as Wendell Gilbert. But surely this old man was not its sole inhabitant, not when there was room for so very many.

More towers and holes appeared from the darkness and Albert began to wonder how many levels a place like this might have. How many hundreds of thousands of eyeless men and women could live in a place like this? He looked up at the towers and remembered the way the blind man had scurried across the ceiling like a spider. For people capable of doing that, this city could stretch for miles up and down through the darkness, level after level. It would be perfect for them. There was no need for stairs or elevators. The city could climb higher and higher into the darkness, or plunge into the very bowels of the earth with only the simplest of architecture.

The singing continued. Albert and Brandy could hear it well, although they could not detect its origin. It seemed to be all around them, yet it definitely grew louder as they followed the blind man.

"I think I can make it out," said Wayne, listening. "But I can't understand it."

"I don't think there are any words," said Albert.

"It's strange," Brandy said, trying to hear the notes. "Pretty."

Yes. It was pretty. Albert was finally beginning to recognize it as the voice of a woman, soft, gentle, voluptuous. Lovely. It was a soothing sound, like a wonderful lullaby.

Ahead of them, the blind man had slowed. They could hear his labored breathing. Finally, he stopped and knelt upon the stone floor. "Go," he told them, the word released in a puff of exhausted breath. He lifted one hand

and pointed straight ahead. “That way. Go to her.”

Her?

“Do you need help?” Albert asked him.

“Go,” the blind man said again.

They went, asking no more questions, and left the blind man in the darkness.

More towers appeared from the gloom as those behind them disappeared back into the darkness. They circled around another hole in the floor, careful not to step too close to the edge. The singing grew louder as they walked, yet they still could not tell precisely where it was coming from.

They pushed forward, ever deeper into the city, closer and closer to its heart, where something new awaited them. Albert squinted into the darkness as something appeared, a pale form rising from the floor. It was now that he began to hear another sound, one separate from the faint singing that had been growing in volume. It was the sound of splashing water. The mysterious figure descended from sight and he realized that the trickling sound was coming from the same place.

“What is that?” Wayne asked. “A swimming pool?”

The form rose again and Albert squinted into the darkness, trying to see this figure in the weak reach of their flashlights. Before he could get a better look, however, the figure dived down beneath the surface again and vanished.

The singing, however, never stopped.

"Another blind man?" Brandy asked.

Albert didn't know. He kept his eyes fixed on the pool. He could now see that there was a short set of steps rising up from the floor. Perhaps the pool was actually a fountain. He wondered absently if it was the city's water source. It made sense that it would need one, after all. As strange as the eyeless man was, he doubted if he could live without water.

As the four of them climbed the steps to the pool, the singing abruptly stopped. The silence that followed was as thick as the stone from which the city had been built. Then a voice came out of the silence: *Welcome*. It was the lovely voice of a woman, the same voice that had been singing just moments before. *I'm so pleased to finally meet you.*

The voice was unlike that of the blind man. His was

hoarse and forced, as though he rarely used it. This voice was soft, elegant, gentle, like a soothing storyteller.

They turned and looked around, searching the shadows with their flashlights. There was no one in sight and the voice seemed to have no origin at all.

"Who are you?" Albert asked loudly. His heart was pounding in his chest with the excitement of being in this city and the uneasiness of being in the presence of this unseen woman. A moment later, his voice came back to him, echoing back from some distant wall.

He looked down into the pool and saw the pale form lying motionless at the bottom. How long could this person—or whatever it was—remain down there?

Though they had no way of knowing this, each of them felt that the woman had just smiled. *I have no name*, she said at last, and that pale form stirred at the bottom of the pool. Albert's eyes followed it, as did the others'. *The man who led you to me has no name, either. No one here has ever had a name. Even this place has no name.*

Albert stood silently, listening. He wanted to ask how that was possible, how any civilization could exist without names and titles. These were the very foundations of language, but he felt somehow that the answers would come. The others stood around him, equally silent, as he stared at the pale shape in the pool.

But you've given my city a name, the voice said. *The City of the Blind, just as someone else once gave our guardian beasts their name.*

"The hounds?" Albert asked, although he found he didn't need an answer.

Yes.

The water in the pool was moving, he saw, softly rippling. A hole in the rock a few inches below the surface, nearly large enough for a person to swim through, was allowing fresh water to flow into the pool. It was as though the temple had been designed with its own kind of indoor plumbing. Perhaps it was an irrigation system of some kind, channeling the water from an underground river. He looked out at the gleaming water beyond, wondering where the outflow was. It had to go somewhere or it would overflow.

You may give me a name, too, the woman said, speaking to Albert. The figure beneath the water moved toward them, and he forgot about the mechanics of the pool. For a moment it became still again, crouched beneath the water, and then it rose and broke through the surface with a soft splash that was surprisingly loud in the silence that surrounded them.

The woman climbed from the water and then stood dripping before them. Her body was long and lean, unnaturally so. Albert saw that he did have a name for her. As soon as he saw her, he knew exactly who she was, who she *must* be. *For you, my dear Albert, I am The Sentinel Queen.*

She stepped toward them. Her entire body was elongated, stretched, well over seven feet tall with arms that reached nearly to her knees. She was naked and hairless, completely bald from head to foot. Her breasts were turned upward, her nipples nearly an inch long and fully erect, pointing not out, as Brandy's and Nicole's did, but at the ceiling. The undersides of her breasts were round swells of firm flesh. As she stepped closer, Albert noticed that her genitals were likewise elongated, her vulva actually dangling between her skinny thighs. She did have a face, unlike the sentinel statues in the temple, but it was a very faint face. She had no eyes, not even the shallow sockets the blind man had. Her brow was smooth and featureless, like the statues, but there was a slight impression of a nose, a small rise in the center of her face, with no nostrils to be seen. Her mouth was a small crease below this, visible, but apparently useless. When she spoke, her lips neither moved nor opened, and it became clear that however she was communicating with them, it was not in the same manner that they spoke to her.

They stared at her, not believing what they were seeing. She was horrendous, a ghastly mockery of nature. Almost everything about her was wrong and yet…

You are aroused by me, she said, sounding almost amused.

The four of them exchanged an uneasy look.

All of you, she explained. *You find me ugly, yet you are aroused by me.*

It was true. Although they each found her repulsive, they could not stop staring at her, as though there were some unthinkable beauty about her. It *did* make them feel strangely aroused to look upon her. Even Brandy and Nicole felt it.

We must hurry. Time is running out. I will explain what I can to you, but you will have to leave soon. She turned and began to walk away from them, around the enormous pool, down the steps and deeper into the darkness. *Follow me.*

Albert, Brandy, Wayne and Nicole followed after her, strangely fascinated by the Sentinel Queen. There was a certain aura about her that was very pleasant, very lovely, as though she were the beautiful goddess Aphrodite, and yet she was…well, she was a *sentinel.*

Albert had never considered that the sentinels were real. He'd assumed that they were merely metaphors of some sort, or at the very least some sort of interpretation of a god or angel. But here he stood, staring at the back of what was undoubtedly an unnaturally tall, naked human with no face.

This place, explained the Sentinel Queen, *is an ancient place. It has been here for ages untold. It was through here that humanity first made its way to the world you call your home. But humanity has always been meant to find its way back.*

"Back to where?" asked Brandy.

Back to where you all came from, Brandy. As if that explained everything, the Sentinel Queen fell silent.

"I don't understand."

Don't worry, Nicole. You will.

"How do you know our names?" Wayne asked.

Dear Wayne, she said, as if his question amused her. *I* know *you. I've been watching you all for a long time.*

"Why were we given the box?" Albert asked, unable to wait any longer for this answer.

Yes, said the Sentinel Queen. *The Box. I owe you an apology for sending it to you. It was not really the way it was supposed to be done. You were supposed to find your own way here, but time has grown short.*

"Then it *was* you who sent it to us," Brandy said.

I sent it, she confirmed. *Someone else delivered it. Do you know how I'm talking to you?*

"You're in our heads, aren't you?" Wayne replied.

Yes. It's a psychic connection. You see, the place I speak of, the place from where humanity came and to where it should someday return, is a place rich with psychic energy. Over the past few thousand years, humanity has been evolving toward its return there.

More and more people are born with a heightened ability to see without seeing and hear without hearing. Those with very good psychic senses can feel that place from which humanity came. It calls out to them psychically. The world's most powerful psychic minds have been drawn here throughout history, obsessed with finding that place that calls to them.

Albert remembered the bones in the decision room. Those were some of those psychic minds, he realized, and perhaps whatever poor souls had traveled here with them.

One such person was Wendell Gilbert. But the road to this city, what you call the Temple of the Blind, was designed to keep these people from returning prematurely, because they are not the ones who are meant to return. Throughout the temple there are psychic guardians, horrific beasts bound in a higher plane. Only the psychic can see them and only the psychic can be harmed by them.

"That's what killed Beverly!" Nicole exclaimed. "She said she was psychic!"

That is correct, said the Sentinel Queen. They had

walked beyond the sight of the pool now. Towers rose around them, empty and gloomy. On their left, a great hole plunged into the darkness below.

"Is that what killed Wendell Gilbert, too?" Albert asked. He remembered that the chamber beyond where they found his body was almost identical to the one in which Beverly had apparently lost her mind. And there were no apparent wounds on his body to indicate a physical attack of any kind.

That is also correct. Wendell Gilbert was obsessed with this place, but he could not get through it because of the thing that killed Beverly Bridger. For most people, psychic or not, that would have been the end of it, but Wendell Gilbert was not just a psychic. He was also a genius. He entered the temple for the first time when he was only twenty-two, and he spent the rest of his life trying to find another way in. He was a brilliant architect, and over the next forty years, he honed his craft into the tool he needed. He built Gilbert House as a shortcut to bypass the temple, the city and the road beyond, but he made a grave miscalculation.

"That forest," Albert guessed, "with all those things

in it."

That place does *have a name. It translates simply into "The Wood." It surrounds the place Wendell was trying to reach. When he discovered his error, it was already too late. He bricked up the first floor to keep out the things in the Wood, but he couldn't keep everything out. One of the things that got in was the beast that attacked you, but there were more. Beverly Bridger could not enter Gilbert House because of what lives on the fourth floor.*

"What lives on the fourth floor?" asked Brandy.

If you wish to keep your sanity, you do not ever want to know.

Brandy shivered. They had made it all the way to the third floor of Gilbert House. What if that thing had not attacked them? What would they have found on the next floor?

"Why was Beverly afraid to touch me?" Albert asked.

The Sentinel Queen shook her head. *That I do not know.*

Albert lowered his eyes to the ground. That seemed

grossly unfair. Was the only person who could answer that question now dead?

When Wendell Gilbert failed to find another way in, he came back to the temple to try again.

"How did he get so far," Nicole asked, "if he couldn't get past the thing that killed Beverly?"

He went the other way, replied the Sentinel Queen. *He went through the labyrinth.*

"How did he do that?"

That I also do not know. Perhaps it was merely luck. It does not matter. He is dead now and can do no more harm. But the harm he's already done is much worse. Gilbert House is closer to that place than the temple is. It is a shorter road. It gives off stronger psychic vibrations, so more psychic minds are able to hone in on it. They will come and they will probably die.

"Can we destroy it?" Wayne asked.

That would be a very bad thing.

"What do you mean?" Wayne didn't understand. How could destroying that place possibly be a bad thing?

Gilbert House is a doorway. If you simply destroy it, you throw open the door.

"And those things in the Wood come pouring out," deduced Albert.

At the very least, yes. The world would be consumed by those that walk the Wood. The greater threat, however, would be that the delicate fabric between this world and that, already damaged where that structure stands, would be shredded completely. The end result would be that your world, smaller by far, would ultimately be swallowed by the Wood.

"That…would definitely suck…" Wayne agreed.

It has happened before, the Sentinel Queen informed them. *To other worlds. It is a terrible fate*. She continued to walk. She did not turn to look at them as they spoke, but Albert felt that she was watching them nonetheless. He could feel her looking at him, examining him, even with her back turned.

Psychic minds of higher sensitivity cannot pass through this world, she continued, *yet it takes a psychic mind to feel the way, to pick up on the negative vibrations of the traps and the positive vibrations of the correct path. To pass through the temple, you must have a perfect balance of psychic and natural skills. Though everyone is a* little *psychic, there are few people in this world who have that perfect balance. You, Albert and Brandy, are two of them.*

"Wait," said Brandy. "You mean I'm psychic?"

More so than most, replied the Sentinel Queen. *But less so than others. The fact that you are still unaware of your psychic abilities makes you stronger, more stable than more powerful psychics. That is why I chose the two of you. Nicole and Wayne, by contrast, possess weak psychic minds like the majority of your species. That is why it took them much longer to hear my singing and tune in to me.*

'*Your species*,' Wayne thought. It was hard to believe he was hearing this.

"So why the box?" asked Albert. "Why not just tell us?"

I'm allowed to interfere very little. I would not have sent you the box at all had time not been running out for us down here.

"What do you mean?"

Many millennia ago, humanity first passed through this city's north gate. There were fourteen of them. All were women. All were pregnant. Thirteen passed through the south gate on their way to your world, which was still new. The last stayed here in this city and gave birth to me. She died when I was still very young and with her died much of what was known about where those women came from. I then gave birth to the people of the City of the Blind, men and women without eyes, who maintained the roads to the south and the north. At one time I had many thousands of children, enough to fill every chamber of this city. She gestured at the empty towers that rose up around them. *But time was not as lasting to them as it is to me. The man who led you to me is the last of his kind and he is very old. When he dies, so will I, and the City of the Blind will again be empty. When that happens, it will crumble. So will the gates and the roads. Humanity will no longer be able to return to its rightful place. I spent a great many millennia waiting for someone to return, but the way back was too difficult to find. Over the centuries, the temple has become hidden. The original tunnel no longer exists. The entrance became lost in the jumbled labyrinth of tunnels beneath your city. I began to fear that no one would ever come, and then my entire existence would have been for nothing. Therefore, Albert and Brandy, I took the risk and I did what was in my power to contact the two of you.*

"What risk?" asked Albert. "Why were you not allowed to do more?"

I am not allowed, replied the Sentinel Queen.

Albert opened his mouth to ask more, to tell her that she had not answered his question, but she stopped and turned to face them. The sight of her naked body was almost startlingly erotic, and yet she was grossly deformed. *The north gate is straight ahead. You must hurry. I hope I've been helpful to you.*

Albert stared into the darkness that must have been north. "But how did you get the box into my car?"

The psychic part of the mind is very susceptible to suggestion, the Sentinel Queen told him. *Neither of you locked your doors on the day you received your item because I told you not to. My son took the two packages to an open grate near the campus and a man named Peter Yowler picked them up and delivered them to your unlocked cars at the specified times. Peter is a sweet man whose brain was badly damaged in an accident when he was only a child. He hardly knew he was doing it. If you found him and asked him today, he wouldn't remember a thing.*

"I see," said Albert. He was actually a little disappointed. He had imagined so many things since receiving the box and the answer seemed so simple, so… *ordinary*. "And when you say that the psychic part of the mind is susceptible to suggestion…did you help me solve the clues on the box?" He remembered feeling as though something was nudging him toward the final clue when he discovered the number twelve panic button outside Juggers Hall. And then there was the way he had known somehow to knock down the wall at the temple's entrance.

A little, admitted the Sentinel Queen.

Albert nodded. He wasn't sure how to feel about that. On one hand, it seemed like such a violation, and yet the thought that she'd been watching over him was also somewhat comforting. "But those phone calls," he remembered. "Why did you call us to Gilbert House if this was where we were supposed to be?"

I was not calling you to Gilbert House. I was calling

you here, away *from Gilbert House.*

Albert glanced at Brandy, confused. "Then you didn't send us the envelope that told us how to get into Gilbert House?"

No. The envelope was Beverly's, not mine. It was her obsession alone that brought that place into your lives.

"But she said she didn't send me the envelope. Who did?"

I do not know.

Again, Albert felt frustrated. It was like Beverly intentionally left him without all these answers. "And what did the gold mean?" he asked. "Why were we given those gold coins?"

Those were just pieces of metal to us. I sent them to you as a thank you for coming, even though you didn't finish. I had hoped that it would bring you back again someday. And if not the coins, then perhaps the sight of my son would keep the Temple of the Blind in your thoughts until you were ready to return. Now hurry! The road ahead will be dangerous, but you've proven yourselves worthy by navigating the temple.

But Albert stood his ground. "Tell me why we had to

give up our clothes," he said. "That man…your son…told us that the hounds could smell them, but you know that doesn't make any sense."

It is the way it is done. The water here has a special quality that helps. The rest is faith. It always has been.

What the hell did that mean?

Now go.

"Go where?" Albert asked. "You haven't told us where we're going. What are we supposed to do?"

You must find the doorway. It is the key to the future of your entire world.

"I don't understand."

You will. Now go.

Albert hesitated for a moment, wanting to ask more, wanting to know more. There was so much he didn't understand, so much she was refusing to tell them. But at last he began to walk. He was not sure why, perhaps it was that psychic suggestion she'd mentioned, but he believed the Sentinel Queen, and he trusted her. And he was certain she'd tolerate no more questions. Brandy and Nicole followed after him.

Not you, the Sentinel Queen said, and Albert and the

girls turned to see that she had one grotesquely long hand clamped onto Wayne's shoulder, holding him back. *You have something else you must do.*

Wayne looked up at her, surprised, and then looked at the others. "But…"

I'm sorry, said the Sentinel Queen. She was talking not to Wayne, but to the others. *I must take him away from you. You must make the trip without him.*

"Why?" asked Wayne, confused.

You must take a different road.

"Why?" asked Albert. He did not like the idea of losing Wayne. Wayne was big and strong and intelligent. He needed him to help keep Brandy and Nicole safe. After all they'd been through, he wasn't sure he could do it by himself.

Because Olivia needs him, she replied.

"Olivia?" Wayne could not believe his ears. "She's still alive?"

She is now. But I can't say how long she will be safe. You must rescue her. She's alone and frightened in a very dark world where she does not belong.

Wayne looked at Albert, his eyes bright and hopeful,

but unsure.

"Go," Albert told him. "If she's out there, you have to bring her back."

"Please, Wayne!" Nicole begged him.

It will be dangerous, said the Sentinel Queen, *but he is capable of surviving on his own and you are more than capable of surviving without him. Now go!*

Albert, Brandy and Nicole turned and headed toward the north gate.

The Sentinel Queen led Wayne west. For a long time they walked in silence, passing empty stone towers and wide, shadowy holes, until at last the city's outer wall appeared. *That is the first seal*, she told him, pointing toward a great slab of stone set into the wall. *This passage travels under the Wood. Its only name literally translates to "Road Beneath the Wood." It was long ago sealed with fourteen seals, one for each woman who passed through the north gate. I will travel with you past this one, but not past the second. I don't know how many seals are still intact. Some day, the things that exist in the Wood will break through them all. They are desperate to get out. They want to come to a living world, but they must never be allowed to do this. Before that happens, the road will have to be destroyed, and there will no longer be a road to the Wood. Not from here, anyway.*

The seal was a half-circle of thick stone, twelve feet high. There were a number of markings on it, but none of them made any sense to Wayne.

Watch, said the Sentinel Queen, and placed the palm of her grotesquely long hand inside a circle on the left side of the seal. The great stone slab moved effortlessly away from her hand, turning like a revolving door on its center and opening onto an earthen tunnel the same shape and size as the seal. The Sentinel Queen urged him inside.

Several yards ahead, there was a second seal.

Listen carefully, said the Sentinel Queen, gripping his shoulder for emphasis. Always close one seal before opening another. Never linger long in one place. Do not touch the roots of the trees that grow in the Wood. If you see something in the darkness, do not investigate it. If anything should call your name while you are down here, do not answer. You must ignore these things. When you pass a stone marker in the road, you must not look back.

This is important. No matter what you hear or feel, you must not look back. You must not stop walking and you must not run. Do nothing but walk straight ahead until you pass the second marker. If you fail to do this, you will die. Only after passing the second marker may you look back. The things in this tunnel are imaginary as long as you don't prove them otherwise, do you understand?

Wayne nodded. He was suddenly very afraid. He wished he didn't have to travel this road alone.

Good. The Sentinel Queen tugged at his shoulder so that he would turn to face her.

Looking up at her, Wayne felt uncomfortably aroused. Looking upon her was like seeing some personal fantasy acted out before him in perfect detail. He could not believe that something so repulsive could be so stunningly sexy.

Good luck, my dear Wayne. Before you go, I have something to give you. A gift from me.

Wayne had not realized just how aroused he was until she took hold of him with her long, bony fingers. *Oh God!* he thought as he felt her gentle caress. He was fully erect, almost *throbbing* against her warm hand. His heart began to pound. He wanted to tell her to stop, but all the strength had run from his body. All he could feel was that part of him she held, the part of him that sent shockwaves of pleasure straight up his spine and into his very brain. What was going on? What was she doing to him?

In his mind's eye, he saw Laura Swiff, slowly peeling off her shirt, revealing her round, heavy breasts, seductively licking her lips. The Sentinel Queen moved closer to him and he actually felt Laura's breath upon his neck, then her lips. He was horrified, almost repulsed, but he was also turned on, more turned on than he had ever been in his life. He felt the Sentinel Queen put her free hand behind his neck as the strength left his legs.

As he felt himself being lowered to the floor, he actually saw Laura crawling toward him on her hands and knees, completely naked, a hungry gleam in her muddy eyes. Then he was inside her. He was inside Laura. He was inside the Sentinel Queen, yet they both seemed to be one and the same. Laura arched backward on top of him, her hands clawing at his chest, wildly enjoying the feel of him inside her and he marveled at how magnificently sexy she was. Then he saw not Laura but Nicole, her pretty, dark eyes staring down at him, so kind, a sweet smile upon her face as she bent forward and kissed him. But when she pulled away, it was neither Laura nor Nicole, but Olivia, so pretty, so sweet. He was not inside her, was not having sex with her. He was only holding her. She was still dressed, still innocent. There were tears in her eyes. She needed him. She needed him to rescue her.

"Are you here to save me?"

He felt dizzy. Darkness swirled around him, swallowing him, and even as his heart broke for Olivia Shadey, he felt something like an orgasm erupt somewhere deep within him.

Then there was only darkness.

Chapter 20

The north gate was identical to the south gate, a stone archway covered in carvings of human body parts tangled together in a strange orgy of existence. Albert stood staring at this gate, his girlfriend on his right, his best friend on his left, unable to stop wondering what terrors may await them.

"Are we ready?" he asked.

"Have we been ready for anything we've been through tonight?" Brandy asked him. Her aching feet made the sight of the long tunnel ahead of them almost unbearable.

"Do you think Wayne will be all right?" Nicole asked.

“I hope so,” Albert replied. “It’s up to him now.” He stared into the darkness ahead, anxious about the challenges that must await them. Had he been alone, he might not have had the courage to continue. But he was not alone. He had Brandy and he had Nicole. And he had the Sentinel Queen, as well, it seemed. And if she was telling them the truth back there, he also had something else, a special advantage.

Did he really possess some sort of psychic ability? Did he really have within his mind a natural sense with which he could read the psychic vibrations within the Temple of the Blind? He remembered the first time he came here, and how he had been convinced that there must be something more to the hate room. That paranoid feeling ultimately saved Brandy from falling into the horrible trap that would later claim Beverly Bridger. Was that his psychic connection? Or was that the Sentinel Queen nudging him in the right direction?

“What do you think is up here?” asked Brandy as she pulled another clump of dried mud from her hair. The stench of that sludge still lingered on her skin.

Albert shook his head. He had no idea. There were

still so many unanswered questions. He reached out and took Brandy's hand. Nicole took his other, wrapping his whole hand in her small fingers so that he could still hold his flashlight.

Together, they stepped through the archway and left the City of the Blind behind them.

ABOUT THE AUTHOR

Brian Harmon grew up in rural Missouri and now lives in Southern Wisconsin with his wife, Guinevere, and their two children.

For more about Brian Harmon and his work, visit www.HarmonUniverse.com

Made in the USA
Middletown, DE
10 August 2019